BARCELONA PLATES

BARCELONA PLATES

ALEXEI SAYLE

SCEPTRE

First published in 2000 by Hodder and Stoughton
A Sceptre Book
Hodder and Stoughton
A division of Hodder Headline

10 9 8 7 6 5

A CIP catalogue record for this title is available
from the British Library.

Typeset by Palimpsest Book Production Limited,
Polmont, Stirlingshire
Printed and bound in Great Britain by
Clays Ltd, St Ives plc

Hodder and Stoughton
A division of Hodder Headline
338 Euston Road
London NW1 3BH

For Linda

CONTENTS

1. BARCELONA PLATES   1

2. MY LIFE'S WORK   19

3. BACK IN TEN MINUTES   29

4. THE MINISTER FOR DEATH   53

5. YOU'RE ONLY MIDDLE-AGED ONCE   81

6. NIC AND TOB   97

7. BIG-HEADED CARTOON ANIMAL   113

8. LOCKED OUT   129

9. MY SHRINKING CIRCLE OF
   ACQUAINTANCES   139

10. THE BAD SAMARITAN   157

11. THE GOOD SAMARITAN   163

12. LOSE WEIGHT, ASK ME HOW   169

13. THIS STUPID SMILE   181

14. THE LAST WOMAN KILLED IN THE
    WAR   199

BARCELONA PLATES

Barnaby's girlfriend thought the funniest thing in the world was people being killed while they were on holiday. She didn't mean the ordinary sad dull stuff: stabbed for a camera, strangled by a British squaddie, gassed by a water heater. Rather it was the ludicrous, the silly, the pointless death that she found hilarious. A German holiday-maker trampled to death by an elephant in the middle of the opening shindig for a new supermarket in Phuket, Thailand was a particular favourite. The elephant, part of the grand opening ceremony for the supermarket, was spooked by an over-enthusiastic clown. The German had only stepped into the supermarket to buy some diarrhoea medicine. That kept her chuckling for weeks. She once told Barnaby's parents about her favourite dead-on-holiday story while they were having Sunday lunch in a bad strange Italian restaurant in South Wimbledon. There she was cackling and dribbling her food over a story about some French couple who'd drifted out to sea on Lilos from their Club Med beach in Corfu and reached the (then but no longer) Communist Albania's territorial waters where they were machine-gunned by a Coastguard boat and died. She could hardly talk for laughing.

She was right though, his girlfriend. There is something sad and touching and vulnerable and pathetic about going on holiday, a triumph of hope over common sense. You imagine just because you've gone to Egypt that you're going to somehow have a great time. But look around you idiot, look at the other idiots being herded on and off buses to go look at old stones. Nobody is having a great time, certainly not the Egyptians and they're in Egypt all the time. If you manage to get killed in some odd and ignominious way and become the stuff of anecdote-telling in bad restaurants in strange suburbs that just about serves you right.

Barnaby knew he'd made a terrible mistake coming on holiday as soon as he read the Comments book in the villa. He'd come on holiday after he'd split up with his girlfriend. He'd split up with his girlfriend after she had accidentally taped a hundred and twenty minutes of their life. They had lived together for five years and had both thought without ever actually discussing it that they would marry at some point. She was an English teacher in one of those inner London further education colleges that mostly seem to exist so black boys can smoke dope in the foyer and pick their girlfriends up after or in the middle of class in old Ford Escorts with black-tinted windows so they can't see where they're going even if they weren't stoned in the first place.

Barnaby's girlfriend wanted to tape a play off the radio which was a two-hour monologue concerning the travails of a girl who was a sexually abused sickle cell anaemia sufferer to discuss with her class at a later date. So she'd dragged out their old Sony portable stereo, plugged it in, tuned the radio to Radio 4, found a C120 tape, started it when the play started and turned it over fastidiously after sixty minutes. But instead of pressing the button that would have taped the play she pressed the button that activated the built-in microphone and recorded a hundred and twenty minutes of hers and Barnaby's home life, which aurally consisted of, 'Want a cup of tea?' 'No thanks.' And a muffled fart while she was out of the room. That was it. That was all. They thought they were happy but the tape told a different story, the tape proved them wrong. No one who lived through a hundred and twenty minutes of such torpidity could be happy. Theirs was a life of grinding tedium. Two weeks later, Barnaby's girlfriend began an affair with a fireman who specialised in dangerous chemical spills. They thought they'd got over that after writing to Zelda West Meads, the advice columnist of the *Mail On Sunday* who is a trained counsellor. But the advice didn't stick. Barnaby's girlfriend was still full of dissatisfaction. 'I want to change the world!' she shouted in Pizza Hut, 'I want to make a difference.' They knew she'd have to do it without Barnaby because they both agreed that he would never make a difference.

Now Barnaby, feeling that he could do with a holiday, was in this bloody villa. He'd found it on the internet 'A charming small village house, in the hamlet of Chite, nestling in the valley of Lecrin. 25 minutes from the ancient city of Granada.' He'd flown into Malaga on a charter flight and picked up a hire car from a cheap Spanish firm. The car he had rented was a class B car, Volkswagen Golf, Renault Clio or similar; his was a white Fiat Uno Turbo. The only odd thing about this car was that although it came from Malaga airport it carried Barcelona number plates. Barnaby noticed stuff like that, that a Madrid car's registration would start with an 'M', a Seville car's would start with a 'Se' a Valencia registered car a 'Va' and so on. Barnaby's car's started with a 'B' for Barcelona. Most of the cars round the villa's way were 'Gra' for Granada but Barnaby thought that 'Cra' for craphole would have been better.

The house had been advertised as having three bedrooms which there were – they were just on top of each other, a pile of shoeboxes stretching up a precipitous staircase. There was also what the people who rented it called a plunge pool, a fetid tiled washing-up bowl and mosquito motel laid into the tiny patio at the rear. Not that if he had wanted to sit up to his waist in green algae could Barnaby have done so because, although it was boiling hot everywhere in the house, the patio was in the shade and somehow managed to be sub zero so that the pool was freezing.

It was the Comments book that really did it though. The villa had a folder in which visitors were invited to record their comments and they did, not letting a lack of insight, talent or intelligence get in their way. Most either had had or

6

pretended to have had a wonderful time. Several had written what they thought were poems.

SPANISH THOUGHTS FROM HOME

I am in England now, and home
And see familiar faces once again
And face the journey of the daily train
Yet even so, my heart is still in Spain.

Little children there are playing in the dust
And grapes are hanging thickly on the vine
And lemon trees are growing in the lane.
God give that I were back with them, in Spain.

Still I can hear the laughter, see the smiles
That brighten up each brown and friendly face
White shining teeth and fiery flashing eyes
And nut brown skin of children, slim and lithe.

Yes I will pack and hie me to the plane
To get away from cold and cloud and mist
Back to the land the golden sun has kissed
To find my heart, which lingers still, in Spain.

Only Americans were frank in writing of their disappointments: 'The town of Niguelas is dirty and dusty, with a cinema. The bars are OK if you don't mind being intimidated by the whacked out locals,' wrote one. Another had obviously had the worst time of his life:

This is our first trip to Europe from the US and we've really enjoyed staying here. We've had some trouble adjusting to the time difference and this has resulted in our not taking advantage of all the things available. For example, our first day here we wanted to got to the Alhambra so we set out for Granada at 10.30 a.m. Once we got in the car I realised that my watch read 4 p.m. (I had been looking at it upside down). Holy week is a tough time to try to see the Alhambra. We spent a few days just walking around Granada and that was a lot of fun. We haven't adjusted to the food too well. Our first night here we ate at Bar Garvi and we recommend avoiding it at all costs. The food was terrible and even though we were starving we couldn't eat more than half of it. In order not to seem rude we asked the barman to wrap the uneaten portion of the food to go. He literally dumped all the food into a plastic bag (we couldn't stop laughing). Eating at home and at McDonalds in Granada were the culinary high-points of the week.

The processions during Holy week are all pretty much the same so, once you've seen one, you've really seen them all. Some guys that look like refugees from a Klu Klux Klan meeting lead the way, they are followed by a statue of Jesus, a marching band and a statue of the Virgin Mary. The band plays something that sounds like the theme to the movie *The Godfather* and it's over. I think that the best part of this trip was the fact that I was able to spend some time with my wife and daughter, without any interruptions from the telephone or television. So don't feel bad if you don't get to see and do everything you planned on doing and just enjoy the time you are able to spend with each other.

Those puppies wouldn't be leaving the good old US again anytime soon.

One of the things that shocked and depressed Barnaby about himself was how much he missed the telly. Back at home, time had been a strong, hard-sided box into which it was impossible to fit all the busy things in his life: home in time for Channel 4 News, out again to the pub or the pictures or the Hampstead Theatre Club, not forgetting to tape *Frasier*, *Red Dwarf* or the footie to see him to bedtime fuzzed from the drink or buzzed from the play. Then Sky News or *The Big Breakfast* waiting to greet him in the morning with its merry chatter. Now time was like a big blue expanding travel bag bought from an airport shop, that could be unzipped and unclipped to reveal a labyrinth of extra pockets and secret compartments . . . there was just no filling the bastard. He now knew what despair was. He now realised it was also a mistake to bring Denmark's answer to *A Brief History Of Time* as his only reading. He also missed eating with other people. Now Barnaby didn't have a problem with eating alone, he quite liked it in fact; when his firm sent him to Manchester or Leeds he was dead happy sitting in a hotel restaurant with a book in front of him, an international man of mystery in his own mind. What he did mind was being the only person in the entire echoing restaurant, always. The Spanish ate so late at night, possibly 2 or 3 a.m. (he had seen a poster advertising a kiddie's puppet show that started at 1.30 a.m.), that there was only ever him and some yawning waiters in there. He got the consumption of a three course meal with wine down to twenty-three minutes.

So what did he do to pass the time? He drove. It filled the day. Day two of his holiday he got in the Fiat and went 200 kilometres to Jerez, stopping only for some fuel and a plate of blood sausage. Barnaby soon figured out from the looks he got from other drivers on the narrow roads around Chite that the southern Spaniards of Almeria province ('Al' plate) didn't like Catalans from Barcelona in their crappy Fiat Unos who thought of themselves more as hard-working North Europeans rather than feckless Latin Southerners.

As soon as Barnaby became aware of this tribal tension he took great pleasure in driving as badly as he could (and it took some effort to drive badly enough to stand out), knowing that each enraged driver, terrified pedestrian or frightened child that he passed was thinking 'Catalan cunt' as he hurtled past them in a cloud of exhaust fumes.

Day three he got to the Northern industrial city of Valladolid before grabbing a plate of tripe and heading back, a round trip of fourteen hours. On day four he got to the capital Madrid in under five hours. Just north he stopped for fuel. In the café attached to the gas station there was a shop section where Barnaby decided to buy a picnic: rough paté, fresh bread and big tomatoes, then it occurred to him that a nice knife would go well with the picnic, so he could sit in some field chopping at his food like a real peasant bloke. Luckily, all motorway cafés in Spain have a large display-case featuring a grand selection of evil-looking blades in a variety of styles and colours. Indeed Barnaby could swear he'd seen a knife-vending machine in one twenty-four hour bar near Guadix. He chose a traditional locking knife made in Albacete, the handle curving inward in a vaguely Moorish way to disguise the true length of the enormous chromed blade that snicked in and out with a truly satisfying 'kerchick'. He took the E90 north-east of Madrid and at the seven hour mark hit Zaragoza. At this point on days one, two and three he would normally have turned back but the thought of another evening sitting in a silent restaurant, indulging in a solo fast-eating contest, pressed him further on. Turning eastwards onto the A2 he hit the Catalan coast just above Tarragona and turned due north. Now he was amongst his own Catalan people, every car here carried Barcelona plates. He stopped at a restaurant called Via Venetosomewhere in the centre of town. He wanted to try the most complicated dish on the menu having already sickened of the plain mountain food of the south. He finally settled on 'aspequenos calabacines en flor en salsa de higado de oca', which is tiny flowering zucchini in a goose liver sauce. He sat happily smiling at his fellow Catalans (for they eat earlier in Barcelona) and then tottered out to the Fiat. He didn't know what to do next – it was too late to head back to Andalucia, so he said to himself 'press on'. North again he drove and the French border soon came up at La Jonquera. He filled up at a Shell station on the edge of the town; there was something familiar about the place. He remembered what it was. When he was in his early twenties and pretty poor he took a package holiday with his then girlfriend to Spain. Two weeks half board in the Hotel Relax on the Costa Brava, travel overnight by coach and all for sixty-five pounds. Not being able to afford the price of meals at the café stops along the way, they had made themselves several huge packed meals. They knew from bitter experience that they needed a lot of food because when they'd been on coach trips before they'd eaten all their sandwiches before the coach pulled out of Victoria bus station. In fact, sometimes just the sight of a bus would send them rushing home to build huge doorstoppers which they would gobble as they made them. So after a tiring overnight ride they had changed coaches at La Jonquera and astonishingly they still had some grub left. Slightly fuddled from lack of sleep Barnaby had sat down on a wall to finish his last tin of pâté and clumsily knocked the tin, a metal plate and his penknife off the other side of the wall, where they landed twelve feet down in a tangle of scrub and cactus – there was no way he could retrieve them, so sadly they were left there.

Now he was back at that same service station, could the knife, the plate and the pâté possibly still be there? With surprising trepidation he approached the wall and looked down: sure enough at the foot of the wall still lying amongst the cactus, rusted now and pitted but indomitably still there, was the pâté, the knife and the plate. He felt somehow soothed and moved. He felt for a moment that he was standing at the still point in a turning world. He went back to the Fiat and got his camera then leant as far over the wall as possible and shot off a whole roll of film, the flash constantly ripping round the petrol station. The people at his local Snappy Snaps place would be perplexed to see that his holiday photos consisted solely of a load of pictures of some rusty garbage at the foot of a wall. Barnaby also resolved to tell a few friends about his pâté. He was sure many of them would like to make regular trips to say hello to his plate, pâté and knife – after all, that's all people wanted out of a holiday – somewhere to go and something to look at when they got there. Barnaby paid for his petrol and also bought a large straw donkey wearing a sombrero which he stuck on the back seat.

Barnaby travelled through France during the night, stopping only for fuel and a few hours' sleep in a car park outside Lyon – by then he knew where he was going and he wanted to get there as soon as possible. Calais at dawn, Le Shuttle bip bip bip, M20, A20 and he was back home in London by the evening. It was the most extraordinary sensation. He felt light, free, bobbing about like a helium party balloon. Everybody thought he was in Spain for another three days and of course the car he was driving had Barcelona plates and he looked sort of Spanish. He had never felt so liberated. As Arnold says in *Total Recall*, 'Wherever you go on holiday it's still you there on holiday,' though maybe it wasn't

Arnold but some bloke talking to Arnold who Arnold later shot in the head and those may not have been the exact words. Barnaby wasn't Barnaby though, he was some Spanish bloke with a Fiat Uno Turbo. He'd thought for a long time about where he was going to stay as he whizzed through France and in the end there was only one place it could be. He would stay at the Garth Hotel. If you have driven North up the M1 or the A1 from London over the past twenty years or so you will know the Garth Hotel. Even if you don't know you know it – you know it. It is something that has grown with more organic persistence than the sorry trees and bushes that occasionally sprout along the roadside. Hendon Way, between the Finchley Road and the North Circular, feeds six lanes of traffic to and from the M1, it is lined with 1930s houses, many with neat front gardens and nasty modern double glazing. Barnaby had moved down to London in 1970 in a white Simca 1100 van driven by his friend Harry: he might have noticed the Garth for the first time then when it occupied one house on a block of maybe ten houses between Garth Road and Cloister Road. The next time was maybe going back to Hull on the National Express coach in the mid 1970s, he glanced out of the window and saw that the Garth had now taken over a couple more houses on the block, it was growing. So it went on. Stuck in a jam in his company Rover 800 because the IRA had blown up Staples Corner he saw it was six houses. And now it has eaten every building it can unless it starts moving backwards down Cloister Road, which it may do one day. There it sits on the

Hendon Way, a large hotel incorporating the Tivoli Italian Restaurant and the Meridian Conference Suite, but which is still very obviously built out of ten little family houses.

It was round about lunchtime when Barnaby arrived at the Garth Hotel. He was vaguely hoping when he parked his car on the shabby forecourt, amongst many with Dutch, German and French plates, that inside the hotel there would still be the remains of the ten houses as they used to be, that the hotel reception would be in the living room of one, complete with a three piece suite and TV in the corner, that the bar and restaurant would be formed from the dining rooms of a couple of the houses, the guests seated at MFI dining tables, drinks served from a trolley, and that the bedrooms would be just as they were left by the previous tenants, complete with fading Human League posters on the walls and Airfix model planes hanging from the ceilings. It wasn't like that at all: there was a marble floor, a proper reception, lifts, though it didn't feel English, perhaps Jordanian or Slovakian instead.

Barnaby checked in and went up to his room. He didn't have any luggage. He collapsed on the bed, switched on the TV and gorged himself on six hours of Sky News, the Discovery Channel and UK Gold. He watched the same episode of *The Bill*, three times. Then he was ready to go out.

Barnaby was aware that he only had this one night in London, he would have to depart some time the next day if he was to get the car back to the rental place in Malaga in time to catch his flight back to London where of course he already was. No time to lose then and only one thing to do . . . drive.

As he headed into central London Barnaby was aware of a delicious sense of a particular freedom, a freedom from care. Usually he cared when a car shot through the lights, when a driver tossed a fag packet out of the window, when he noticed the crazy leaning angles of the rainforest of traffic lights that clustered at every corner. It came to him that all these years Barnaby had carried an imaginary foreign tourist round in his head and every time he noted some shameful sign of the dirty and ugly life that he and his fellow Britons led then he cringed at what this tourist must think. But now he was that tourist and frankly he didn't give a fuck – sure it was all different to his own Barcelona but he saw it all now, clear and fresh as if for the first time: ragged and spikey, not dirty and grim; funky not fucked up; clued up, not clammy.

Camden Market – look at the drug dealers by the station, that's so cool, you'd have to be a life-denying drip not to find it cool. Barnaby thought he might buy some drugs. The black man took him down an alley handed over the drugs and then he and a friend tried to rob Barnaby but Barnaby pulled out the knife he'd bought at the motorway place outside Madrid and cut them both across the face with two quick strokes, forehand and backhand, swick, swick.

He took the drugs, they were very good, Barnaby could see why people liked them.

Earl's Court, the Fiat parked skewed on the pavement half blocking the Warwick Road, causing such a jam that it got mentioned on London News Talk Radio. In the gay pub a nice-looking Chinese boy caught Barnaby's eye, they went into the cemetery and the young man fucked him quite violently. He could see why people liked that as well. Barnaby shot away in the Uno five seconds ahead of the police tow truck, he didn't give a fuck. Soho, no not good enough at all, clerks in raincoats clutching beer bottles by the neck, standing outside bars looking desperately up and down the street as if good times were about to arrive in a mini cab. Not good enough at all. The Walworth Road, better. The blue steel glint of gunbarrels in the light brown public bar. Pint after pint of chemical-tasting lager. It does the job, nothing to be ashamed of there, why should some snobby foreigner sneer at it, he'd get his fucking face pushed in if he did, even with that knife in his belt.

Hanway Street, Little Spain, 3 a.m., the shebeens where the finished-duty Spanish waiters are always glad to greet a fellow countryman. The Garth Hotel 6 a.m. Back on the road at check-out time and in reverse: A20, M20, the Shuttle, the N3 through northern France; he got confused on the périphérique and found himself heading through central Paris, pushing it now and heading south almost by smell. His girlfriend had told him he would never change the world but he had gone one better and changed himself. Hitting 120 kph on the Champs-Elysées, skidding on the cobbles round the carousel and down the avenue Franklin D Roosevelt. As he hit the place du Canada and swerved on to the cours Albert 1er, a black Mercedes 280 with four people aboard swooped past him doing about 150 kph. Underpowered for such a big fat car. The light little Fiat caught the limousine as they dove side by side into the underpass under the place d'Alma. Driving like the insouciant Catalan he was, the straw donkey rocking about on the back seat, Barnaby pulled ahead of the Merc, then with a flick of the steering wheel changed lanes without warning, clipping the front bumper of the bigger car. Its lethargic balance upset, the Mercedes wobbled then ploughed into the thirteenth stanchion of the underpass and span round losing speed and bits and pieces of itself, as Barnaby tore up the other side and out into the Paris night. He didn't give a fuck.

MY LIFE'S WORK

I should have been an architect. That's what I was training to be for seven years. Except the Architectural Society's Christmas Revue was one of the lowlights of the academic year so a girlfriend persuaded me to write some sketches. Everybody at the Archi Soc thought the sketches, mostly about mullions and architraves, were absolutely brilliant so I sent some ideas up to BBC Radio 4's *Weekending* programme. This was a show of brain-bending unfunniness whose unfunniness was excused by the fact that it was supposed to be 'satire'. When you listened to the credits it seemed to have been written by about a hundred blokes. They must have done a word each. The producers used a tiny bit of what I did and I started going up to London on my motorbike to attend the uncommissioned writers' meetings, I swear some of those there only came for the free biscuits. Me though, I got on with the thrusting young producers, all planning to get out as soon as they could and get into telly, and after a while they made me a staff writer.

I was twenty-one and a professional comedy writer with my own laminated BBC security pass, my life's work. I got on well with one of the other guys on the staff and we became a sometimes writing team. The two of us put together a script for a TV sitcom pilot and pitched it to a producer at the BBC. He was keen and the thing got made very quickly – we thought that was how it was, you had a good idea, you told a bloke about it, it got made. We didn't know it would never be so easy again. Unfortunately the transmission day of our sitcom pilot was the day of the Dunblane massacre and, because there was a five second scene in our show where a man waved a glue gun around in a post office, the BBC yanked it in a panic and replaced it with a twenty-nine-year-old episode of *Sykes*. Then they couldn't find a slot to transmit it for a year and a half and when they did show it on BBC2, England versus Portugal was on the other channels so nobody watched it, not even my dad. The BBC producer was now an LWT producer anyway so he wasn't interested any more, it never got made into a series.

Meanwhile, I contributed to a comedy show that went out on Channel 4. One of my bits, everybody said, was the most brilliant sketch they'd ever seen: it was a pastiche of those courageous cancer sufferer documentaries, and featured a brave boy who had been decapitated by a charging rhinoceros while on holiday in Kenya and had his head replaced by transplant surgeons with a polished wooden head. The bit was funny and poignant by turns and a certainty for a BAFTA award. However, the day before it was due to be shown, in an incredible coincidence, a woman on safari in Zimbabwe was beheaded by a charging hippo. The TV executives again went into a flap and after half a day of frantic meetings the skit was edited out, in deference, supposedly, to the woman's grieving family who it was presumed would be watching comedy shows on the telly while waiting for their daughter's body to be flown home. When it was considered safe to broadcast the sketch, some three weeks later (perhaps it was thought by then that the family had decided they didn't like their late daughter that much after all), the series had ended and as it never went to a second series, the bit went unseen for ever.

Nearly a year gone by with me writing things that nobody had seen, though extraordinarily I had made more money than I'd ever made in my life and my career could be said in many ways to be going very well. After spending some time not writing for TV I achieved the promotion many writers yearn for and got into not writing for movies. Failing upwards as they say, a vicious climb. I got a phone call from my agent saying that a singer had an idea for a movie and he had suggested I write it. I went to the singer's home on the Thames where he cooked me a lamb curry with saffron rice in a kitchen bigger than the one at the Ritz while he told me about his idea. He was one of those singers that you have only vaguely heard of but who can still sell millions of CDs and fill the Albert Hall for weeks on end. I hated his music myself but a movie was a big step up for me and seeing as his record company had a film division and they'd be happy to blow a couple of million to keep their star happy, it was going to get made. If I turned his barmy, crap idea into something decent it would help my career. At this point there was a talented young director on board, fresh out of film school with a brilliant graduation short behind him. We met many times, laughed at the singer behind his back and together created something very rare and special. Two weeks before the start of principal photography the singer panicked, worried that the talented young director wasn't experienced enough. The singer fired the talented young director and hired a withered old bloke whose only experience of the movies was directing those flat wobbly film inserts for *Dad's Army*. Lunch on the first day's filming took two and a half hours. The movie never even got a cinema release but did, three years later, turn up on a satellite channel called 'Sky Exclusives' where they pretend the flicks they're showing are not feeble junk they've picked up for no money but are just so flipping good that their producers have absolutely insisted that they are not shown in theatres but are instead bounced up into space and then down again into the homes of McNugget eaters all over Europe.

After that my non-career ricocheted between film and TV: I spent a year working on a six part series for Channel 4, commissioned through one of the big independent companies. Me and the guy who would produce it when it got made became extremely close; I was godfather to his second daughter, we talked on the phone every day, until one day we didn't, like he's slid off the side of the earth. I hid outside his house for a morning then followed him down to a country house hotel in Suffolk where he was spending a breakaway weekend with his kids and his wife's family. After I threatened to drive his Renault Espace off a cliff he told me the truth. Turns out the commissioning editor at Channel 4 had been fired and all his projects in development had been cancelled on that same day, regardless of merit – just as the possessions of scarlet fever sufferers were burnt in a previous age for fear of some sort of contamination.

I did some brilliant writing on a documentary about bacon but somehow my name didn't appear on the credits. The series editor said she 'forgot', and it was too late to do anything about it now. The thing won an Emmy. I wasn't invited to the ceremony. Had a fantastic idea for a movie, went to Belgium to pitch it to an enthusiastic representative of the European Film Development Fund. He was mad for it. They paid me a fortune in Euros to do a twelve page treatment. On the day I handed it in, two Hollywood movies on exactly the same subject as my film, with completely identical plots and duplicate endings opened in the States. I didn't know this because I don't read the trade papers. Bumped into the European guy in Wardour Street the next day and he screamed at me that I was a plagiarising thief who had made him look like a gullible fool back in Brussels, he really shouted excellent

English. Over his shoulder I could see Alan Parker and Sir David Puttnam looking at us.

Then a great deal of hard work on an animation series that was supposed to be the British answer to the *Simpsons*, a question as it turns out that didn't need an answer and like all the other British answers to the *Simpsons* it never got made. Then a huge amount of rewriting on a film where the money fell through. Then very quickly a sitcom idea with my partner that was made, was shown on time, was up against very weak opposition and was completely shite.

Eighteen months of no work and clinical depression next before a commission to pen a script for a medium-budget British film. I wrote a script that was my best work by far. The producers loved the script, the money people came on board smooth as pie, a star attached their name, the film was a go go.

Then.

The producer, who'd just had a big hit by accident, tried to get clever. He didn't want a tough director to stand up to him so he hired a woman who had only ever directed a twenty-nine minute short for BBC Wales who he thought could be pushed around, but who turned out to be both stubborn and stupid. She shot whole scenes – and this was a comedy remember – focused solely on a tin of peas. I flew up to the Highlands where they were shooting, at my own expense, to try to quell a mutiny amongst the actors. There wasn't much I could do really except spend the whole night drinking with them in the hotel bar, listening to them whine. The producer came in about ten o'clock, asked for our attention and told us all that he was pulling the plug on the film. If we wanted paying it was now in the hands of the insurance company, who had all the film that had been shot so far and might or might not try to edit it into some sort of sense. I checked out of the hotel early the next morning and was racing back to Edinburgh airport in my rental car, because I had an afternoon meeting with some producers from the American cable channel HBO about writing a biopic of General Eisenhower, when I lost control of the car on a bend, the vehicle shot up a bank and tore through a hedge. On the other side of the hedge was an oak tree. With all four wheels off the ground a branch smashed through the windscreen skewering my chest, ripping through the seat back and suspending me and the car like some car oak nut thing.

I passed out. However, there was a farmer working in the field who used the CB radio in his tractor to call up a medivac helicopter from Glasgow. The fire brigade, who happened to be nearby putting out a blazing barn, cut me out of the car and when the copter arrived I was ready to be flown to the Glasgow Royal Infirmary. There, alternating teams worked through the night using up all the plasma in the hospital and surrounding health district to rebuild my shattered chest cavity, lungs, trachea and spine. With skill, dedication and hard work the surgeons dragged me back from the edge of death.

The cunts.

BACK IN TEN MINUTES

Indicating left and sliding gently into the inside lane in good time Alice turned her little red car (a magnet for squeegie merchants and rose sellers this – a middle-aged woman in a little red car) off the hurtling traffic of the southbound M1 motorway and safely into the Watford Gap service station. She didn't stop and park though, as most do, but kept rolling, nervous but acting all casual as if her bright little car had legitimate business in the wild back part of the service area where the big trucks, their engines always running, crouch on the potholed, diesel-smeared asphalt. She waited off to the side of an automatic barrier until a service station employee in their car pressed a security pass to the gate and activated it. Before it swung closed again she stamped hard on the accelerator pedal and zipped out after the departing car, passing through a very emphatic 'No Entry' sign. (A jolt of nervous electricity right there.) She left the service area and found herself on a narrow country lane lined with high hedges, silent and green, turned left, drove across a pretty hump-backed bridge that spans the Grand Union Canal and after no more than two hundred yards came to a pub called the Stag's Head. She swung into its yard and parked. A very nice pub, several bars, out the back there is a garden planted with clematis and honeysuckle that steps down in verdant terraces to the banks of the canal – you can eat your lunch there, pub stuff and Portuguese food: fresh sardines and halibut Portuguese style, as longboats chugalug by and the M1 roars, feet away, day and night like an angry four-hundred-mile dragon.

Alice enjoyed her lunch. She hadn't eaten since she'd had some Bird's Eye Chicken Dippers for her supper the night before. She had Rissois pancakes, pancakes rolled with prawns in a Parisienne sauce. Then at the end mild disaster struck her one and only interview smart suit, which she'd decided to wear for the journey down. Her hands might have been shaking a bit, sure, but those little pots of half-cream are so damnably difficult to open: result half-cream and suit collision, not necessarily a problem. Slight change of plan needed that's all. The plan had been this . . . she had an interview for the job of head supervisor of the Phomex call centre (which was in a big shed on an industrial park in Daventry, Northamptonshire) on Monday morning at 10.00 a.m. You should know what a call centre is because you will have spoken to one, but you probably don't, so this is what they are. Call centres employ more people in this country than cars, steel and shipbuilding and what they do is this: your TV has broken down so you call the company that sold it to you, a call centre masquerades as this company, they soothe you with palliative words they have learnt from a script, they get on your good side and arrange for an engineer to call, then they try to sell you something. Sometimes the engineer even turns up. Since they use the phone lines it doesn't matter where call centres are, so they are in big sheds on industrial parks and because callers equate regional accents with honesty and decency (deleting from their minds such stout Yorkshiremen as the Yorkshire Ripper and the Black Panther) they are in the North and Midlands. Alice's job interview was on Monday morning and this was only Friday afternoon. Phomex had sent her a first class rail ticket to travel from her home in Newcastle and paid for one night at the Moat House Hotel on the same trading estate outside Daventry. She had converted this into three nights staying at the Globe Hotel in Weedon, Northants, and driven there.

Weedon Northants: an odd place, a place of parallel lines. The primary rail link to the North-west runs underneath it through a cutting in the middle of town; the Grand Union Canal runs above it on an embankment; dead straight Watling Street, the A5, is its high street at ground level. To the north are the remains of Weedon Barracks, begun here in 1803 because it is the central point from any coast: if the French had invaded England, then troops from here would be rushed by the fastest, sleekest canal boats to repel them. Between the railway and canal embankments is the

Victorian church with a Norman tower. Alice cared for none of this because now the town was nothing but antique shops and antique warehouses, a couple of pub/hotels and what were once shops selling useful stuff: fruit, nails, butchers, corn chandlers and grain warehouses, all now selling nothing but old junk. Alice had been hoping to squirrel away the weekend poking and prying round every single one of the stalls. She had a large collection of what she thought was called Devon ware. What was once cheap seaside souvenir pottery in a rather fetching blue and white and sold for pennies, had in the last few years become a minor craze and she wanted to find out what sort of prices pieces of it were fetching. First things first though, she had to find a twenty-four-hour dry cleaners and she did. There was one right in the centre of Weedon between Shabby Genteel and Bitz'n'Bobs, surprising really but undeniably there in a town that couldn't carry the weight of a papershop. 'M. BIFTONI, DRY CLEANERS, (24-hour express service available)'. She parked the car in a bay away from the screaming traffic and took the suit into the shop. A pleasant, small, brown-faced man came out of the hiss and steam of the back when she stepped on the mat that had an electronic buzzer built into it laid across the entrance.

'Hi,' said Alice, showing the stain – half-cream in the shape of the Isle of Wight – 'I've got cream on my erm . . . suit and I need it cleaned by erm . . . tomorrow.'

Presumably he who was Mr M. Biftoni stared at it, professional and concerned. 'Hmm tight deadline.' Then he smiled. 'Won't be a problem.' All this said in an indeterminate all-purpose foreign accent. 'Three o'clock tomorrow?'

Alice sighed with relief. 'Three o'clock's fine.' The man wrote out a blue slip with Alice's name on it and she took it back to the car clutched to her chest and drove round to the hotel. Checked into her room at the Globe Hotel she lay on the bed and masturbated, imagining herself being thrown naked and bound between Johnny Vaughan and the latest female presenter of Channel 4's *The Big Breakfast*. After that she got her lap-top computer out, plugged it into the phone line and dialled up the front page of the *Bradford Telegraph and Argus*. Alice liked to read the local papers of towns she had never been to. For a long time she had had a weekly subscription to the *Banbury Guardian*; she found it soothing to read about vicious fights in city centres she would never walk through and lectures in libraries she would never visit. Plus small-town life still seemed to exist at a gentler speed. She treasured a particular front-page story in the *Banbury Guardian*: 'Sibford Man Loses Camera.' Now that newspapers put their front pages on the internet she could visit ten or twenty towns in an evening.

How does somebody get to be the way they are? In Alice's case it could be said that her main manufacturer was her family's ideology of 'The One Big Chance'. This ideology of the one big chance permeated Alice's family as thoroughly as the theory of the Five Year Plan had once been shot through the People's Republic Of China. Like

Marxism, Alice's mum's theory of 'The One Big Chance' aspired to be both an ideology and a scientific law. Along with the other immutable laws of the known universe – Boyle's Law for the Expansion of Gases and Ohm's Law of Something or Other – there was another law, perhaps vouchsafed only to Alice's mum and certain other pioneers in the field of fucking up young minds, and it consisted of the inescapable and inflexible rule that every person has been allocated (by the same power that decreed that objects fall at thirty-two feet per second and that the current flowing through an element in a circuit is directly proportional to the voltage drop across it) just one big break in life, one opportunity, one big chance. A person has to be constantly on the look-out for this one big chance and must leap on it and seize it when it sticks its whiskery head out of the sewer pipe and if you don't grab it there and then you never get another go. That's it for the rest of your life.

Most ideologies benefit most those who propagate them: just as Stalinism's main beneficiary was Stalin, so Alice's mum's theory reflected best on Alice's mum. Her big break, her gigantic chance, the defining moment of her life was, simply put, Alice's dad. As she told it many times, she had first seen him at a Woodcraft Folk social in the town hall annexe in Manchester and even though he was on the arm of her best friend she knew instantly that this man was the one she had to have and that through him her life would be shaped and defined. The Woodcraft Folk is a youth organisation set up in the 1930s by various left-wing Fabian organisations of the day to counteract the militarist/fascist tendencies of the Boy Scouts, Girl Guides and the Boys Brigade. They formed a sort of paramilitary wing of the Co-op and it was easy enough for Alice's mum to contrive a camping accident that put her best friend in a sanatorium for six months, thus leaving the long road clear to Alice's dad and a life as the wife of a future Executive Officer in one of the largest chemical plants in the North-east, which is pretty much the pinnacle of what any woman could possibly want.

Alice absorbed her mum's ideology like a good North Korean but it did not serve her well. You may not remember the sport of ice acrobatics but in the late 1960s when Alice was a young girl it was very big, indeed it ranked alongside speedway and greyhound racing for popularity and was challenging for Olympic status. Alice wanted more than anything else to be an ice acrobat. On her bedroom wall she had posters of the now forgotten stars of ice acrobatics: Barry Poole and Sonia Harvey-Michaels. She practised and practised and made it through to the regional ice acrobatics finals. This she thought was her big break. Then, ten minutes before she arrived, the traditional bus-load of old age pensioners with its dodgy brakes crashed into the lobby of the sports hall killing the judging committee, the national secretary of the ice acrobats association and the British team. Parallels were drawn with the Munich air crash but really it was worse: the sport never recovered and neither did Alice. She felt her big chance had come and been cruelly snatched from her. From that point on nothing interested her much. She drifted through school and then drifted through life, unsuitable men came and went until before she knew it she hadn't had sex for ten years and was assistant supervisor of a call centre on Teeside.

Alice spent the next morning rooting round the antique markets. She found two pieces of blue Devon ware: a jug with 'A Present from Exmouth', on it which was going for four pounds and a coffee mug that simply said 'Philip', was asking two pounds for itself. She smiled to herself and might have made a small buzzing noise (she'd been doing that a bit lately). Her collection was both beautiful and, as it turned out, something of a sound investment. For lunch she had a beef and ale pie in the other posh pub in Weedon, the Heart Of England. Then at 3.05 p.m. she strode confidently up to the door of M. Biftoni Dry Cleaners, laid her hand on the knob and pushed. It wouldn't open. She pushed again but it wouldn't open. Then she saw a handwritten sign stuck to the glass inside the door: it read 'Back In Ten Minutes'. Oh well, ten minutes wasn't long. Alice went away and stared at the menu in the Riverside Chinese takeaway on the other side of Watling Street where Roman Legions had once tramped. They were asking £1.70 for plain boiled rice. Alice would generally pay £1.50 or less for rice from a takeaway, and she thought £1.70 was too much – she'd only pay that for pilau rice because that was yellow and had bits in it. Alice looked down the road at all the antique shops that used to be other shops, at least they were still selling something she thought. Where she lived shops were always closing down and when they did, when a shop went out of business and its sign was taken down, there was no clue to its former identity so that after a few days it was difficult to remember what kind of shop it had been. Was it a butcher's? A massage parlour? A Tamil bookshop? Who knows? Once it was gone it was almost impossible to recall what was there before. The only way you might find out is if you used to shop there regularly and after a few months you noticed you were totally out of Tamil books so you realised that must have been what the place sold. Alice wondered if the same phenomenon would occur with a really famous building like the Houses of Parliament or Sellafield? If they took all the signs down saying what it was, would you walk past thinking: 'Now hang on, something used to go on in that big Gothic Revival building, some sort of circus was it? . . . No, can't remember.'

Alice worried a lot about shops. If she found a nice, well-run shop, she often never went back there in case she became too attached to it When she had fallen in love with a shop there always seemed to come a horrible day when she'd turn a corner to find it had closed down because the lovely couple who ran it had been killed in a car crash and their only son was in an ashram and didn't want to be a butcher, or the Council had put up their rent by 500 per cent or an out of town superstore had opened nearby, or something like that, there was always something like that. Alice also worried about restaurants. She noticed that at failing bistros a waiter would often stand in the doorway looking up and down the street with an incredibly mournful expression on his face. Alice reckoned that if you wanted to get the punters flocking into your café then stationing a manic depressive in the entrance wasn't the right way to go about it. Finally, when the place did inevitably go under, the owners never seemed to say so right out. What they did was to put a handwritten notice in the window saying something like 'Restaurant closed for redecoration/refurbishment – grand reopening in three weeks'. The notice would still be there, yellow and withered, several years later. She didn't know why these owners put up the little notice – was it some pathetic piece of self-delusion, that maybe somehow their Icelandic Cod Brasserie would be resurrected? Or was it, as seems more likely, a feeble attempt to put off all their creditors for a couple more weeks?

Round the corner from Alice's flat there was a stationery shop that had gone bust. In the window there was a notice written in felt-tip pen on an old envelope saying 'Shop to Let – Enquire at shop next door.' Then there was an arrow pointing to the shop next door. The shop next door was a Halal grocers which had also gone out of business and in its window was another note in ink saying 'Shop to Let – Enquire at shop next door' and an arrow which pointed straight back to the empty stationery store. Several times she had seen potential lessees of the shops stuck like a wasp against a window, buzzing backwards and forwards from one sign to another.

It was 3.20 p.m. and she was back at the dry cleaners. Still nobody there. Peering through the glass she could see her suit hanging behind the counter on a rail with a load of other clothes. It was in a clear plastic bag looking very neat and pressed and the hanger it was on was one of those chunky plastic ones that you usually only get if you opt for the gold service, not a crappy wire one. This was obviously a good dry cleaners, if you could only get at your dry cleaning that is. Alice went into Shabby Genteel, next door, at 3.35 p.m.. A woman was sitting at a desk at the back of the cluttered shop.

'Erm excuse me,' said Alice, 'I've got some dry cleaning in the shop next door, and there's a note on the door saying back in ten minutes, but it's been at least half an hour now and nobody's come back . . . erm yet.' Alice was aware that waiting only half an hour before making a fuss was probably considered a bit precipitate these days: time seemed to have become more elastic, more Jamaican or Arabic, in the last few years. If a washing machine was to be delivered in the morning that meant it would come in the afternoon or possibly the next day, service technicians were the same and builders of course, by and large, never turned up at all. The entryphone in Alice's block had been broken for months, it didn't ring. Workmen had come to fix it four times but each time had gone away because they got no reply when they rang the entryphone. It drove Alice mad but she knew from many uncomprehending conversations that it didn't bother lots of people at all or they had once cared but had taught themselves not to. So Alice was a little tentative about bothering the woman, but her reply still came as a bit of a surprise.

'Hmmm funny that,' said the woman, 'I was in the Wheatsheaf over the road last night and I noticed Mr Biftoni was working late, cleaning stuff till about half eight when I looked, he's usually gone by five or six. Then when I came out of the pub at eleven I noticed that that sign was already in the window.'

Alice couldn't understand it. 'What? He put a sign saying "Back in ten minutes" in his window over fifteen hours ago!'

'Seems like it,' said the woman, who seemed to be taking a certain relish in the situation. They both contemplated the strangeness of this for a couple of minutes in silence.

'Err thanks,' said Alice and left the shop to stand staring at the dry cleaners for nearly half an hour as trucks and cars whipped by. Round about four o'clock a young man drove up in a Land Rover, parked and came and tried the door. Eager to enlist an ally Alice went up to him. 'There's nobody there,' she babbled excitedly, 'apparently there's been nobody there all day, even though, as you can see, the sign says they'll be back in ten minutes.'

'Aw really?' said the young man. 'Bloody nuisance.'

'You got something in there?' asked Alice.

'Yeah, getting married tomorrow, bloody wedding suit's in there, and the best man's suit come to think of it, and all the bridesmaids' frocks and the Bishop's surplice and his pointy hat thing.'

'Blimey,' gasped Alice. 'Mine's just my interview suit . . . blimey. So what shall we do about it?'

'How d'ya mean?' asked the young man.

'Well, maybe we can find out where he lives or something, this Mr Biftoni. The owner,' explained Alice.

'Oh no,' said the young man, shocked. 'Just have to leave it that's all, not make a fuss, nothing to be done.'

'But what will you do about your wedding suit?' Such calm acceptance in the face of disorder agitated Alice beyond bearing. 'You've got to get your clothes back! I can see them hanging there, I can see the Bishop's mitre, you've got to get the bishop's clothes back at least, those are holy vestments in there!'

'Naw, wear jeans or something,' he was already backing away towards his car, Alice's fervour disturbing his pond. 'Hope you get your suit back!' he shouted as he sped away.

Alice thought for a few seconds then marched back into Shabby Genteel. 'Hello me again,' she said to the woman who was quite enjoying all this, 'you wouldn't know, by any chance, where this Mr Biftoni happens to live would you?'

'Well,' said the woman, 'as a matter fact I do. I sold him a box ottoman for his house a while back and I took it round . . . I've got the address here somewhere . . . it's in a village called Woodford Halse.' She rootled through a card index. 'Ah here it is . . .' She wrote the address on a card.

Alice went and stood outside the dry cleaners for another half an hour then got her car from the hotel car park and drove to the village of Woodford Halse.

When she got to Woodford Halse Alice was faintly surprised to find herself driving through a Northern industrial town plonked down in Northamptonshire. It was a railway town and its builders had seen no reason to alter their standard design just because they were not in the North. Slate roofed Salford terraces ran downhill to incongruous Midlands pastureland, grey-green hawthorn hedged the abandoned railway lines running north, south, east and west, grass grew along the torn up tracks and rabbits waited on crumbling platforms for trains that never came, just like real commuters really. Alice was inclined towards Victorian melancholy, more as a pastime than as a fundamental part of her character, it was cheap and you could do it on your own. She would often stand in a rain-sodden graveyard and a couple of times she had got dressed up in her best clothes and stood in the shadows outside house parties that she had been invited to, envying the happy smiling people going inside to the light and chatter. Alice thought Saturday evening the loneliest time of all to be away from home. She gave herself a thrill of sadness thinking of herself far from home and the life inside the houses – TV on to no one, baths and make-up, clothes thrown about, early tea, empty streets, then she had to stop as real sadness started to creep in. Mr Biftoni's house was in one of the Northern terraces. Alice rapped on the door and heard her knock echo in an empty house. Staring through the grimy front window she confirmed that the place had been stripped bare, grey floorboards and dusty squares on the walls where pictures had been. She got into her car again and drove back to Weedon thinking hard.

Alice lay on the bed in her hotel room. The day before she had bought that month's *Marie Claire* at a motorway service station and amongst the photos of 'thirty-five feminist vaginas' and such there was one of the usual questionnaires, this one, 'How determined are you?' Alice had filled it in that morning and only got fifty points, 'Gibberiing indecisive jelly fish' – she needed at least a hundred and fifty points to qualify as a 'Determinator'. Using the hotel's giveaway pen and carefully copying the typeface of the magazine she inscribed between questions fifteen and sixteen: '15 (a) If you took your interview suit (the only suit that made you feel like a real grown up and not six years old) to a dry cleaners and that dry cleaners said they'd be back in ten minutes but they weren't, would you (a) walk away and forget it – one point (b) write a stiff letter to the Master Dry Cleaners' Association of the UK – five points or (c) break into the fucker's shop and steal your fucking suit back from the cunt – a hundred and fifty points.' Alice ticked (c) so hard she tore through the page, ripping Camille Paglia's vagina on the other side.

Come ten o'clock and Alice was round the back of M. Biftoni Dry Cleaners scaling the wall. She was working very hard at not thinking because she knew a moment's reflection would mean she was lost, back over the wall to the hotel and another nut added to her squirrel hoard of regret nuts, which was creaking the floorboards of the wobbly treehouse, that was her mind. Moreover, there was a strong part of her that expected that, at any minute, something would come along and stop her. Then she could return to the hotel feeling she'd done all she could to get her dry cleaning back without actually getting her dry cleaning back, which ('don't think about it don't think about it, lah, lah, lah, lah, lah') would be what the local papers called breaking and entering. The wall would be too high to climb – it wasn't. There would be a big dog in the yard – there wasn't. The back door would be a solid sheet of welded titanium that could resist being knocked off its hinges by a single brusque kick from a woman whose thighs had been firmed by fifteen years of jazz tap dance classes – it couldn't.

The orange sodium lights of the A5 filtered through the dusty window giving the shop a fishtank glow. With the slow motion of a diver, and as quietly as possible, Alice squeezed past the rows of hanging garments. She felt like she was in some sort of clothes abbatoir: row upon row of dead plastic-wrapped shapes swinging gently as she passed. At the front of the shop was her suit. With some difficulty, hiding as trucks rushed by illuminating the shop, and balancing on a wonky chair, she hooked it off the rail. Clutching it to her she bolted for the back door and that was when the big dog, who had a sense of humour, got her. Or rather he got her suit. Leaping for Alice, his claws ripped into fabric and cellophane, his teeth tore through buttons and cotton. Alice flew like the ice acrobat she had once been in a single bound from the ground to the top of the wall, the dog still attached to her suit. The canine slammed into the brickwork and lost its grip falling back to earth in a flurry of fur and fabric as she dropped into the alley. She was not alone. She'd never had a fight with a policewoman before but in retrospect you'd have thought they'd be better at it seeing as they must spend a lot of time doing it. Not once letting go of her dry cleaning it took three of them to get her into the squad car. That 'Careful, mind your head,' thing that they do also enables them to smack your bonce against the panda's roof a couple of times and Alice got a right old handful of that before you could say she was subdued.

The nearest police station was in Banbury and it was now near on pub closing time. For those of you who don't know English market towns, just let me say that on a Saturday night, once the pubs close, the streets are the province of gangs of young men and women looking for a fight. One of those gangs has blue uniforms, drives around in stripey cars and carries long sticks. A scrap with a mad woman clinging on to some washing had been a nice appetiser but the main battle of the evening beckoned and they were keen to have at it. English men had been doing serious damage to each other on this land since long before and after the Battle of Naseby. The urge to combat seeped up through the ground in these parts along with the radon gas and the coppers had no will or desire to resist.

Alice was cursorily charged with theft and resisting arrest.

A brief, unsuccessful attempt was made to wrest her cleaning off her but she hung on to it grimly so after a while they gave up and she was slung into a cell to await transfer to the County Court. As time crept on towards midnight, more and more casualties were brought in and the police decided to kick Alice out, telling her to appear on Monday for committal proceedings. Thus she found herself standing on a street corner clutching a torn suit, the plastic wrapping flapping in the wind.

Suddenly distance, usually so negligible in the modern world, was a problem for Alice. She was in Banbury, her little car and all her belongings were in Weedon, ten miles away. She had no money, there was a slow-motion riot going on, what was she supposed to do? Walk it like some Thomas Hardy character? Luckily she didn't have to. As she stood there a Land Rover swung up to her corner. 'Hello there,' said a pleasant voice, 'you look a bit lost.' It took Alice a moment to focus on the driver: it was the young man whose wedding suit was in Mr Biftoni's shop.

'No, not exactly lost, no,' she replied with the pedantry of those who have been in a fight, 'see I know where I am, I just don't want to be here.'

'Well it's a figure of speech,' he said. 'Can I give you a lift somewhere?'

'I'd like to go back to Weedon,' she held up her tattered bundle. 'I've got my cleaning back though.'

'Well kudos to you,' said the young man obviously not convinced that it might have been worth it. He leaned over and opened the passenger door. Alice climbed in and they drove off. 'I'm Guy, by the way,' he said.

'Alice,' she replied.

Guy put the clumsy old car in gear, swerved round a couple of young women rolling and biting each other in the middle of the road and accelerated. Soon they were out of town and on a narrow country road, the hedges flicked past, faster and faster in the headlights. 'Couldn't get another bloody suit,' he said.

'Pardon,' said Alice.

'Suit for the wedding,' he said. 'Here, how did you get your cleaning back? Did the shop open?'

'No, I broke in and stole it back.'

'Going a bit far that,' he replied after giving it a moment's thought.

'Do you think so? I think it might just have been the most important thing I've ever done. I think I might just be striking a blow against some nameless evil. I think this might be my big chance.'

'It's just shopping,' said Guy.

'It's not just fucking shopping, Guy,' she said with such seriousness that Guy pressed harder on the accelerator, all the quicker to get her out of his car. 'Every time somebody gets bad service and accepts it, every time somebody has something lost by a shop and lets it go, every time somebody waits in for a service engineer who never turns up and shrugs their shoulders to another wasted day, then maybe there is another bit of the stock of human pride that is lost, a fraction of our resistance to injustice that is rubbed away, a teeny bit of our individuality that is ground into the mud.' She turned to face Guy. He had always thought that the phrase 'her eyes burned', was only an expression, now he knew different. 'There is something coming Guy, something is coming or maybe it's already here, I don't know. I do know that it's something very bad, something that we need all our pride, all our resistance to fight but we can't see it because we've been inoculated by all the Mr Biftonis. Oh yes, I'm sure there's more than one of them! We've become desensitised by all these missed appointments, all those appliances that expire the day after the guarantee is up, all those call centres that keep us hanging on for hours. Oh Christ, I was part of it!' She started talking in a voice that Guy recognised from a hundred calls to computer helplines and insurance companies, 'If you want your spirit broken press one, if you want to hear Greensleeves for the nine hundredth time press two!' She was shouting now. Guy never knew a Land Rover could go so fast and he was never so glad to get anybody out of his car as when he dumped her off at her hotel and resolved never to offer his help to anybody ever again. You were better keeping yourself to yourself, that was for sure.

At 10 a.m. on Monday morning the selection panel at Phomex International in Daventry, meeting in the big boardroom to fill the post of head supervisor, called its first interviewee: Alice. Though they were seeing other candidates, they had pretty much decided, on the basis of her references and CV, to offer the job to her. That was before they saw her. She strode into the big meeting room in her best interview suit. The skirt was torn into shreds so that with every step you got a glimpse of her knickers, like some mad semaphore message flashing over and over again 'pants . . . pants . . . pants . . .' Her jacket hung off her shoulders in stripes interwoven with bits of clear plastic wrapping, giving a good view of her grimy bra. She took the seat that was offered and sat pleasantly waiting for the panel's questions.

'So Alice,' said the head interview woman feeling a little floaty herself at the strange sight of Alice, 'what do you feel you could offer Phomex as head supervisor of our call centre?'

'Nothing,' said Alice.

The panel looked at each other, what was this? Some kind of new interview tactic they were teaching at business school? Alice stood up, all the men shifted back slightly and all the women leaned forward. She spoke to them all in a firm, just a bit too calm, voice. At the end of her speech she was shouting.

'I wanted to tell you, it's only polite after all,' a sudden swerve, 'you can't have the rail fare back though. After this I'm going to London. I'll get all my savings out of the building society and I'll get a loan and I'm going to open a shop. Yeah a little corner shop. I don't know what I'll sell yet, something useful to people though, something that's hard to get these days like hardware or fruit and something. Now when I've got my little shop it stands to reason OK? I'll have to go to the bank with the takings or somewhere sometime. Have to close it then won't I?'

That seemed fair enough to the panel, she'd have to close it unless she had an assistant, those were expensive and anyway she didn't seem at that point to be the sort of woman that anybody would want to get within two hundred miles of.

'So I'll close up the shop but I don't want to send customers round to the competition do I? 'Course I don't. What I'll do is I'll put a sign on the door, a sign that says "Back In Ten Minutes".' She was yelling now and spitting a bit, '... and you can bet that when I say on that sign that I'll be back in ten minutes then I ... will ... be ... back ... in ... ten ... minutes!'

(Or maybe eleven) she thought to herself.

THE MINISTER FOR DEATH

There's some things, they say, like swimming or riding a bike, that are supposed to come right back to you even after years not doing them. I would add killing to that list. There I was, seventy-two years old and lying on the pavement with me steak pie, chips and curry sauce, tightly wrapped and warm like a pet on me chest. 'Please son,' I said, 'I've got me pension. 'Ere in me back pocket, please take it son. Just don't hurt me son. Don't hurt me.' I was whinging on like an awld geezer is supposed to. He was standing over me waving a kitchen knife about. I reached behind me into me pants and pulled out the Tokarev army pistol that I'd taken off of the body of a dead Chinese officer in Korea all them years ago and I shot the lad, twice, upper body, bang, bang. Like they taught me at the public expense back in Aldershot in the days when. We both lay on the ground, nobody came to look, the streets were empty and the sound of gunfire wasn't so unusual, late at night on Netherfield

Road, North End of Liverpool, that you'd get up from the telly to take a look or ha! ha! phone the police. I climbed slowly to my feet, took a look at him curled up there on the wet pavement, went home and ate me supper.

I was halfway through me meal when I realised something: this food from the chippy tasted better to me than food had tasted for years – either the Wing Yip had shipped a gourmet chef over from Singapore or it was killing the lad that had done it. I noticed I felt light as well, light and fit, bendy and . . . young. The aches and pains of years had slid off me, was that what it took? All those who went to gyms, started affairs, joined clubs, gave up jobs at the Water Board to teach geography to cystic fibrosis sufferers in Malawi when all they needed to do was to whack a few strung-out smackheads, who frankly the world could do without.

I felt like some sort of old lion raising his giant head and sniffing the wind, this was still my territory. Or rather it had been my territory and now it was again. I've lived round this part of Liverpool all me life and some obscure stubbornness has made me determined to stay, though anytime I wanted I could have skedaddled over the water or gone to Ormskirk with the woollybacks or somewhere. No, I wanted to walk the same streets I'd always walked, to drink in the same pub, to go to the same shops, no matter how much had changed. Except, stupidly, it had all changed, every molecule of it. In the 1960s they had planed the streets down, back to the same contours it had had when it was farmland in the

1600s or something. Then they put some stuff back, sort of haphazard, a pub for every five pubs they'd knocked down, a shop for every twenty, a tower block where there'd been a street. They'd re-used some of the old street names, though generally not where the old streets with those names had been before. Imagine what it was like for some old person, to find that Opie Street was now a dead end running east to west on a concrete gantry and had somehow shifted half a mile towards the river. I seem to remember that they took the opportunity to change all the bus numbers at the same time.

So it didn't matter that there were the same number of folk living in the area, because all the old ones stopped going out. When they knocked down our old house in Secombe Street the Council put me, me wife and our daughter in one of the tower blocks. Then when me wife died and me daughter moved to Hoylake, over the water, the Council stuck me in these flats exclusively for old people in Kirk Street (once a wide boulevard, now a glass-littered stump) – they thought it was nicer if the scallies had us all in one place, I suppose.

When I got out of the Army, after Korea, I took up me apprenticeship again, pipe fitter welder. Then it was me trade; I was a good worker, careful, meticulous, always kind to me own apprentices, when them things still mattered though, like I say, stubborn, which often put me in bad with the gaffers. And always very particular about me tools: American, I used to like best, you could buy them off the lads who worked on the Cunards, they'd ship them over. There was always something sturdy and timeless about American tools.

I've always drunk in the same pub since I was a lad: The Jester, corner of Netherfield Road and Everton Valley. They knocked it down in 1958 but they put another one up more or less on the same site though at a skew-whiff angle to the road and in the middle of a bombsite – at least they still called it The Jester. It was always an ugly pub and it was always a rough pub, both in its old and new incarnations. As if annoyed with its name, it was also a fucking miserable pub. The violence in there though was like out of one of them books about the history of warfare that I used to get out of the library. For most of the life of The Jester, from when they slung it up round about the time of the Battle of Inkerman, it was only fists and feet and though they can make a right mess of a person you'd have to be pretty determined to beat somebody to death in that organic, holistic, non-mechanical way. The fists and feet era was what you might call the pre-Colombian period, since it was the coming of the drugs that speeded it all up. The kids started using knives and clubs and stuck to them for a fair while; I heard some middle-aged beer-gut holder waxing lyrical about the innocence of those days at the bar the other day. But you can't stand in the way of progress. Chapter three 'The Invention of Gunpowder', single-barrel poachers' guns, aged things nicked from farmhouses out Ormskirk way, soon overtaken by sawn-off shotguns; over and unders and five-shot pumps to be worn under an Adidas shell suit. At the time of my little addition to the crime statistics, we are bang up-to-date: Glock 9mm pistols, H&K MP 35 sub-machine guns, ready and waiting for the twenty-first century. If a shooter is hanging up in the armoury of any modern police force in the world, then it's also hanging about in The Jester.

I stopped fighting myself a little before the end of the feet and fists period. Before that I'd been one of the hard men in a hard pub. I was one of the little ones you didn't worry about until you suddenly found yourself in an argument you couldn't back out of, then, 'Oh shit, oh shit, how did you get here?' You were going down in a mill of fists, blood ballooning from your nose as you tasted floorboard and a steel-toed boot smacked the side of your head. I told meself I gave up scrapping because I was thirty-five with a wife and a kid on the way and scrapping was for the young 'uns but if I'm honest a lad gave me a terrible hiding one night, no worse than I'd handed out to others mind, broken rib, fractured cheekbone from being kicked in the head, split lip. So I gave up. Still it was my local boozer, I'd sit in the corner, quiet with me pint of Guinness, I was never much of a talker. Thing was, though, as the years went by it had got much more dangerous to go out. I got mugged twice at closing time in the last six months, before I got the Tokarev out of the shoe box on top of the wardrobe, where it had been for forty years. I stripped it down, cleaned it, oiled it and stuck it down the back of me pants. It made me feel safe but I don't think I ever once considered using it, not on the surface anyway, but there seems to be a lot going on with me that even I don't know about and you don't do a thing like that without a reason, do you?

My home help brought me the the *Echo* the next morning. The work of the night before was front page news: Orlando Stokes, unemployed, aged nineteen, found shot dead, motive unknown. Mind you, there's only one motive these days round our way. Though by accident I'd managed to put an exotic spin on a fairly common story. See, the Tokarev takes this ancient Soviet ammo, rimless 7.65mm round it's called. From this fact some Merseyside copper who'd been on an advanced paranoia course at Hendon Police College broached the theory that the feared Chechen Mafia might be making an attempt to take over the North-west drug scene. A couple of days later, an Opel Omega full of Swiss tourists on their way to Anfield for some neverwalkalonery caused panic in Great Homer Street when they stopped to ask directions and their 'CH' plate sent all the scallies diving into doorways and running home for their nine mils. Thing of it was though, I scanned all the articles about the shooting, and nowhere did I get a mention. I'd been in The Jester and he'd been in The Jester, I'd been in the chippy and he'd been in the chippy, where there'd only been me, him and a couple of kids for God's sake. Still nobody mentioned me. At first I was dead relieved, I'm very good at locking unpleasant thoughts away in little rooms but I'd had to take the idea that the police were about to come for me, down a corridor, out of the door and then drop the idea in a lake where it had still kept bobbing to the surface shouting its head off. After that though I was amazed to find that I felt insulted. Insulted that not one person had remembered seeing me. What was I, Scotch mist?

Yes I was, I was invisible and I had been becoming invisible for some time, another word you might use for invisible is 'old'. It starts when you are round about thirty-five that you start to slip from view, thinning along with your hair, transparent patches growing with each day. By sixty-five you're pretty much see-through. If you're reading this somewhere public now, look up quick, see all the old people you hadn't noticed before, they're all over the place, there's fucking millions of us. You don't see us because you don't want to fuck us. That's the long and the short of it. I've watched a lot of them animal documentaries on the Discovery Channel, and pretty much everything comes down to sex in the end. Not sex exactly but reproduction, the survival of the species. Like when that lad gave me the going over, it was just the same as when the old bull elephant gets fucked over by the young buck. Nature's way of saying, 'Sod off pal, your old faded sperm ain't needed around these parts.'

All these youngsters simply hadn't seen me, I didn't appear on their radar screens, I was a stealth codger, they didn't want to fuck me and I wasn't going to stop them fucking anybody clse, end of story. Sure, Orlando had seen me, had dimly taken me in because he was after me pension, he had a reason, a motivation, a need, but as for the rest . . . nothing. That made me angry and it spoilt me life, me food started tasting like dog biscuits again and me sciatica came back. How dare they not see me and report me to the coppers and get me arrested for murder, how dare they! Every night I was in that bleeding pub, most nights I was in that chip shop, all right, I didn't draw attention to meself, OK, I wasn't one of them pub characters or anything, not one of them old people who manages to not be invisible by eating their hat or weeing themselves or organising outings for kiddies with terminal illnesses or something. I was always polite, paid for me beer, said please and thank you, good manners, and look where it got me. Ignored.

I am selfish, I am cruel, I am extraordinarily pleased when a young person gets a terrible disease or a school bus goes off a cliff, if I was not weak I would wreak such terrible revenge. In other words I am an average old person.

I am not weak. This clever clockwork killing machine, the handgun, my trusty Tokarev, gives me power. I will not go back to the way I was. CNN provided the answer, one of the pieces they trot out from time to time is how the ex-Soviet Mafias are taking over all the crime in Europe. Russian crims taking over the Cyprus Banking community, the Côte d'Azur now a base for Georgian and Kazakhstan gangs muscling into gambling, drugs and prostitution with incredible violence, Ukrainians bribing state officials in Hungary to turn a blind eye to their white slave trade and finally, as a sort of comical footnote, the activities of a gang in the UK from a small not yet independent Republic. In the old Soviet Union they'd been involved in frauds connected with sheep and that was more or less it but in Britain they had tried to blackmail a footballer from their own country who owed them a fortune in gambling debts to throw a match. Amazingly, and nobody expected this, he'd gone to the police, influenced by his English girlfriend whom they hadn't taken into their calculations. The gangsters were encouraged to place huge bets on the game then the player went out and scored a hat trick. The gangsters were allowed to watch themselves losing hundreds of thousands of pounds on Sky Sports then the coppers burst in and they were arrested. There was a tape of a group of thickset men being bundled into a police van looking ashamed and angry. 'There are,' I thought, 'some people I could work with.'

The only place old folk like me have figured in big time crime is when we get used as drug mules. They say we don't know where anything comes from these days: people buy their meat from the supermarket wrapped in clingfilm because they don't want to think it's dead animal they're scoffing, but those trendies in them clubs in London should stop and think that the toot they're snorting has come into the country up the arse of some old age pensioner on a free round-trip to Amsterdam. That wasn't what I was after though. First stop was the library in Great Homer Street. I'd never used the Reference section before but it was easy to figure out. The next day I went into town and got a couple of hundred quid out of the building society then I went to Lime Street and, using me Old Person's Rail Pass and waiting till after ten thirty for an off peak return, I got the train to London Euston. They didn't have an embassy because the Russians who were in alliance with the Armenian minority were still trying to hang on to the place and there was the usual berserk civil war going on, but I had found the address of a 'friendship society' in a place called Wood Green, which was up the Piccadilly Line almost to its end. After all, if you want to open a business venture with a foreign country then you go to the embassy trade department or its nearest equivalent.

There was a big brick pyramid called Wood Green Shopping City, which seemed to have sucked the life out of all the little shops around it so that most of them were some kind of charity shop, some were charities for countries and some were charities for diseases and some were charities for countries with diseases. The friendship society was one of these, inside were the usual dead people's hats, plus some badly carved mutant folk dolls and tins of what I think was some kind of food or maybe varnish (you couldn't tell from the photo on the tin) called Pallkacky. Around the walls were posters in the kind of colour that seemed to be black and white, depicting the country's few sites of interest and the few things they used to make before everything fell apart.

I haven't been to London much but a thing I've noticed about the people there is that they look much more like characters out of films or on the telly – people in Liverpool just look like people, if you know what I mean. The woman who ran the friendship society looked like the joke wife of a vicar in one of them bad sitcoms they say they're not going to make any more. Thick glasses, a cardi knitted out of some sort of industrial cabling, a grey paratrooper's helmet of hair. She told me readily enough that she had gone to Russia in the mid 1960s, in the good old Kruschev days, for a conference of 'progressive peace elements', as she called it. During the conference she had fallen madly in love with their leading 'poet' and he in turn had fallen for her exotic charms. (It wouldn't do in The Jester to say you were a poet. In their part of the world though, poet seemed to be another word for psychopath. I don't know, maybe everybody dived out of the boozer when Wordsworth came in, but I doubt it.) The Russians had made him their puppet minister of culture (in charge, mostly, of puppet shows) then he'd had a row with the puppet president, who was also, in the way of things over there, his cousin. He became a fervent nationalist and took to the forests blowing up Russian troop trains, killing all the survivors and sticking their heads on poles, while his wife waited back in Hornsey, keeping the flame alive. He was lured into a fatal ambush by a half-sister on New Year's Day 1975. On the walls there were some posters of his poetry that she had translated into English, it seemed to be mostly about eagles.

We had to dance a fair bit around the houses before I could make it clear to the woman who it was that I wanted to meet and of course I had to give her the two hundred quid I'd got out of the Northern Rock. She thought she might know some of the people involved and she'd like two hundred more quid if it came off. She promised to give me a ring by the middle of the next week. As I was leaving she pressed something cold into my hands, 'A taste of the homeland,' she said with a mad smile. When I got outside I saw that she had given me a tin of sardines caught off their toxic coast. The tin had a picture of her late husband on it.

I went home, bought an answerphone machine from Dixons and waited. I didn't go out much, I thought I might as well stay out of The Jester, no point in jogging anybody's memory there, which just left the library.

The woman from the friendship society phoned two and a half weeks later, ten days after she said she would but like any convert she'd become more like them than they were themselves, if you know what I mean, and I've since found there's no point in going on to any of them about time-keeping, they're a nomadic tribal people and you don't have to get your goats to market bang on the minute like.

Their office was in a place called South Mimms, which you have to get a train to from the middle of London, above a row of shops, lots of TV cameras everywhere and them ugly concertina security grills on all the windows. They wanted me there at eleven o'clock so I couldn't get the cheapest city saver fare, though I didn't get seen till after one, poor time-keeping you see. And the young man that I talked to wasn't exactly at the top of their organisation but he had insight: he saw who I was, I wasn't some old duffer in a flat hat and an M&S wind cheater to him, I was me,

I could do things. He admitted quite readily that they did have a problem in the area under discussion, he said it was expensive for them to ship their own people in and out of this country and when they got here they lacked intimate knowledge of the terrain. They had tried local subcontractors but their experiences had not been happy ones. I could see he took me serious, they've got poetic souls you see and they respect the old – in their society the ancients have wisdom and many of their fiercest warriors would be eligible for a bus pass in our country. My new friend, Ruslan, told me that what I should do was do the first one for free, a sort of sampler, and if that all went well then they'd see what they could do. That was very fair of him.

The target was also a young lad. I was glad of that, I wanted them all to be young lads. I was given a photo, and a home address. Ruslan told me that he was the youngest son of one of those South London families that had been at it since the time of Dr Johnson. He was in charge of their drugs operation, something that my new friends would like to take over, he was also cautious, very rarely went off his home ground and he knew people were after him. A difficult target. I went back to Liverpool that day and got all me savings out of the building society. A thousand pounds, this would finance my new career.

The territory his family controlled was a large slice of south-east London. I went down the library and looked up where he lived. I imagined the rest of his family lived in the houses they had always lived in or maybe big executive jobs in a forest somewhere behind high walls but he chose to live in a converted warehouse right on the Thames in an area called Rotherhithe. The map in the library also told me that there was a big hotel right next door. The Holiday Inn, Nelson's Dock it was called. I rang them up and booked a room for a week, they told me I could choose the room when I got there. I took the train to Euston, then a tube to London Bridge, from there there was a little water-taxi that took me straight to the hotel's own pier. Before I chose my room I took a look at Canada Wharf – sure enough the underground garage of the block was reached by an automatic gate that was overlooked by an arm of the hotel. I booked a room with a good view of this gate, stationed myself by the window with my binoculars and waited.

I first saw him about 5 p.m., slowly rolling down the street in a black BMW 3 series. I had already figured that he was very vulnerable when he swiped his card to open the car park gates, but he knew that, so he kept the car gliding slowly along until there was nobody near, then he swung to the gate, quickly ran his card through the lock then drove on through to safety. I quickly got to know his routine: during the day he came and went at odd hours but night-times he would generally leave at nine and return between two thirty and three, sometimes with a girl sometimes not. Even though it was late at night he observed the same security routine, nevertheless this was the time I decided I would do him.

I figured there's only one thing more invisible than an old man and that is an old man with a dog. There was a big supermarket development nearby called Surrey Quays that had a noticeboard by the check-outs, some old lady who was going into a home where they wouldn't let her take her dog, I convinced her I would give it a loving home. After that I walked my dog down the street every night, coinciding with him two nights out of three. He never gave me a glance. On the fourth night I shot him in the head twice while he was unlocking the gate, then I turned down on to the river path, found a quiet place and shot the dog. I picked it up and chucked it into the Thames. If somebody had dug the slug out of the dog they could have made a match with the lad and Orlando but they don't do autopsies on dead dogs. The police National Computer did kick out that the strange ballistic used in the Rotherhithe shooting was the same as in the Netherfield Road killing and, coppers being greater fantasists than science fiction writers, they put poor stupid Orlando at the nexus of some conspiracy linking Merseyside, the Caucasus and Rotherhithe. In a way they were right.

A while back I mentioned that me home help brought me the newspaper and perhaps this is a good place to go into more detail about these girls, the only companions of my twilight years. When I retired from the building sites I managed to convince our old quack of a GP that I'd got multiple sclerosis. The silly old twat signed me off for a nice little disability pension and the Social Services, considering that I was crippled, allocated me home helps twice a day for an hour in the morning and an hour and a half in the evening to cook, clean and generally care for me. Say what you like about Liverpool but they still try to keep the flame of some sort of Socialist paradise flickering. They also gave me a pendant to hang round my neck with a button on it that when pressed dialled up an emergency number at a charity in Vauxhall Road. When I started making some money I had this button set in a silver surround of my own design, strung from a silver chain. There were loads of girls that came and went, all of them lovely and all of them kind and gentle, cleaning up spew and piss and comforting the mental, day in day out for shitty wages. The Good Lord seemed to reward them for their unstinting benevolence by giving them the most tragic personal lives this side of one of them daytime soaps. 'Hello Maureen,' I would say as one came through the door. 'Are your brother's test results back yet? . . . Not good eh, it's spread to his liver, oh dear . . . well it's your day to clean my lavvy. Thanks a lot.' 'Hello Doreen, was your uncle in the car when they dragged it out of the canal? . . . Your twin cousins as well? Oh dear . . . well I think I fancy a nice piece of boiled ham today.' My main two were Maureen and Irene; it didn't take them long to figure out that I was swinging the lead but they didn't turn me in; a visit to my flat was a nice break for them from the unrelenting misery of their regular customers. It was Maureen though, a faded woman on the edge of retirement, who was the nearest thing to a friend I had back then. I liked her because she was friendly, kind and intelligent and she liked me because I didn't drool and shit my pants. A sound basis for a relationship. Maureen was mad about the movies or the 'fillums', as she called them. Too mad I thought. I had all the Sky Movie channels so we would often sit together in the evenings watching some piece of crap that was on at the cinema three years ago. I sat through them, though they made me angry sometimes. I can't see the point of made up stories: while I do watch all the films they show, I prefer the documentaries or the sport. Like there'd always be some detail in a fillum that really annoyed me, for instance we was watching that flick *Nikita*, on Sky Movies Gold with that Bridget Fonda in it and she's supposed to be doing what I had recently started doing. Now her bosses, this shady government organisation, want her to hit somebody in a crowded restaurant, so what gun do these professionals give her? A Desert Eagle 9mm, which is a piece of Israeli shite anyway, it's a huge magnum pistol that weighs a ton and the one they gave her was, get this, chromed! Chromed! So it's all bright and shiny and reflects the light all lovely like! Just in case anybody has happened to miss the sight of this nearly naked beef toting a cannon the size of an outboard motor around a swanky restaurant. Her Grandad Henry wouldn't have used anything like that, a Colt .45 man if I remember right from *Jesse James*, and *How The West Was Won*. See, a bit of reading down the library will tell you that the professional assassin needs a weapon that is one, unobtrusive and, two, reliable, that's all, that's it. The tiny .22 calibre revolver is the choice of professionals, nine times out of ten. I couldn't say this to Maureen, of course, she thinks I'm a harmless old bloke.

Well, I can't tell you how pleased Ruslan was. Very pleased indeed. He gave me a thousand pounds for the lad in South London and another thousand on account for the next one, which was a pleasant surprise. One thing I needed Ruslan to help me with was getting the proper tools for the job. He pointed me in the right direction and for two hundred pounds in a pub down the Walworth Road I bought a little Ruger .22 revolver with black gaffer tape wrapped round the butt, serial number filed off and a clear plastic bag full of ammunition. He offered me a crappy little Spanish Astra but I'd have none of it. My Ruger, this dinky little revolver, American made of course, no bigger than a kid's toy, was the proper tool for the job, the choice of professionals. Like I said I've always been particular about me tools.

From then on, I did about one a month: a 'computer consultant', who'd been stealing off us, a woman who was an investigative journalist sniffing too close to our drugs connection, a couple of Uzbeks who were trying to take over an oil swindle we had going and, a bit of a novelty this one, an Israeli Talmudic scholar who tried to do us on a diamond smuggling scheme. The footballer also got his, one day at the training ground. My friends went from strength to strength – it wasn't so much that our gang was killing people, all the new players did that, with great enthusiasm: some like the Chechens and the Ukrainians used needless and uncalled for brutality as a kind of trademark and the Georgians would always do a rival, his entire family, his pets and for some reason his interior decorator, that was their gimmick. The thing about us though was that we were doing it with such stealth. Targets were being hit by a wraith as far as anybody could tell. I was our gimmick. Them other countries are superstitious folk and they get easily spooked, a little word from one of our people would often be enough to set them on their toes. And seeing as the whole operation was going so well Ruslan got rapidly promoted, he became the head of the firm and the chief of the tribe, at least he did once I killed his brother for him.

Another thing I discovered was music. Irene started playing me all this gear she listened to – Radiohead, Tricky, Finley Quaye – difficult stuff for an old bloke but I reckon these kids had something to say. Now that I had gear worth nicking I fortified my flat in Kirk Street with every security device known to mankind and furnished it with a lot of Italian stuff from shops like Atrium and Viaduct in London plus a big-screen TV and a boss stereo. It might seem funny that I didn't move somewhere that was less in the middle of a war zone – the truth is that I liked my double life, I liked it that nobody saw me, nobody knew my secret. Plus for the kind of butler service I was getting from Maureen and the home helps I would have had to pay a fortune. Of course I was out a lot more than I used to be and I had a lot of great clobber in my flat. I told the home helps I'd won the lottery, that seemed to satisfy them. I gave them spare keys so they could sit in my flat when I wasn't there and watch TV, listen to music, help themselves from the fridge or the drinks cabinet and hide from their supervisor.

I was supposed to sign their timesheets every day to show that they had done the work but if I wasn't there they would put 'unable to sign', in the space and tell anybody who asked that my multiple sclerosis was particularly bad that day.

Nearly a year after I started working for him Ruslan threw a big party at his home and I was invited. For these people to invite you to their home is a great honour. Back home, they told me, life is conducted on the streets and in the coffee houses. For the men that is, even if you go to their homes you never see the women, maybe they're hidden behind the skirting board. The whole tribe was no longer in South Mimms. St John's Wood it was now, a huge double-fronted house with more of those ugly concertina security grills that make every window look like a lift door, big drive, Mercs and Range Rovers parked outside. Guarding the door several burly lads. CID on the street photographing all the guests, a sure sign that we were the happening gang in town. Inside, hundreds of people. Nobody I knew really, apart from Ruslan who was tied up with a gaggle of his family. Of the folk there some were British, local councillors and officials who were in their pay, some women dressed like presenters off of BBC 2's *Newsnight* who must have been from our large stable of high-priced prostitutes, a huge number of men from the home country and over in a corner the woman from the friendship society – the only person at the whole 'do' in national dress. I thought at first she was pulling a car battery apart but as I got closer and heard the terrible racket I realised she was playing a 'native' instrument and singing in the language, presumably one of her husband's songs about eagles. She looked up and saw me, put down her instrument and came over.

'Ah,' she said taking me by the arm, 'the good friend of the homeland. Young Ruslan does not tell me much and I don't want to know but I do believe it was a great day for the home country when you came into my shop.' Honestly, she had a worse English accent, even though she was English, than most of the foreigners there. Then she started introducing me around. This party was being thrown in honour of the government in exile, most of whom were based in London though some had flown in from Madrid and places. It would be a great prize for my friends to get their hands on a whole fucking country. One after another I was introduced to the people who would be in charge of various things once they took their country off the Russians. I met the burger chef who one fine day might be the Minister for Information Technology, the bus conductor destined for the post of Minister for Women's Affairs and Equal Opportunities in the Workplace and the overweight thug bound for the Ministry of Sport.

Now as a rule I don't drink much, I like to keep in control, but they just wouldn't take no for an answer when the vodka came round, it was an insult to the homeland, apparently, if you didn't knock it back in one go, it meant you were in league with the Armenian minority. After a lot of vodkas knocked back in one go my head started to feel light and the yabber of all the guests began to crowd in on me. It was only when I was in such a throng that it struck me that I spent such a lot of time alone and when I did meet people it was mostly because I was planning to kill them. With that thought the faces of those I had shot suddenly came spinning up at me: Orlando, the lad in Rotherhithe, the lady journalist, all of them, their eyes wide as they got popped. It was a bad time for the Undersecretary for the Admiralty in Exile to ask me why I was there. I started shouting 'Me? I'm in the government too, can't you see it? It's all over me. I'm going to be in the government of the sacred homeland, I'm the Minister for Death, that's what I am, the Minister for Death! The Minister for Death! I made all this, me and my clockwork killing machine. I made it all. Me, me!' A couple of the burly lads came over and hustled me into a back room. They shoved me into a chair and I think I carried on shouting for a bit, then after the shouting I did some mumbling. Ruslan entered a few minutes later, he gave me a funny look, I felt I'd let the lad down though right then I couldn't remember why. Ruslan, the burly blokes and an older fellow I'd never seen before had a quick argument in their native tongue then they picked me up again and dragged me out of a rear entrance. They took me to Euston in a Mercedes and put me on the train to Lime Street. I fell asleep on the train and an attendant had to wake me at the other end and put me into a taxi back to Kirk Street. Too much vodka.

It was about a week later, I hadn't heard from them but then sometimes up to a month went by before they got in touch so I wasn't worried. We was watching a film on the TV, me on the couch, Maureen on my Regency leather reclining chair. I noticed this flick that we were watching had an actor called Robert Prosky in it. I said to Maureen, 'That's Robert Prosky that is.' 'Who?' she said. 'Robert Prosky,' I said. 'He took over as the desk sergeant in *Hill Street Blues* after the first bloke got cancer but he's in loads and loads of movies. Every time they need an uncle-ish sort of bloke they nearly always call on Robert Prosky. He's in *Broadcast News*, *Mrs Doubtfire*, *Dead Man Walking*, loads of films that are on Sky Movies.' I was getting quite agitated, worked up even, Maureen was looking at me a bit funny, I guessed she was wondering to herself, as I was, why I knew so much about this potato-faced old Polish bloke, so I let myself plough on, I'd found this was the way I would generally answer myself. 'See Maureen, I've got a theory, there's loads of young ones around, young actors, if they want a teenager they've got millions that can do the job really well but when there's an oldster needs playing then there's much less choice. There's only a few actors of my age around who aren't fucked up physically with all the millions of diseases we get or mad or drunk or too set in their ways that they can't take on board new things. Robert Prosky's one of them. He's old but he's fit, he's not nuts, he can remember his lines, he can do the job. He's a rare thing Robert Prosky is. A valuable commodity.' So that's what I was going on about . . . I stopped speaking and there was a long silence. Maureen really seemed to be thinking very hard about what I had said. I was pleased she was taking my philosophising so serious.

'Yeah Ronny,' she finally replied, then she reached over to the side of the chair and pulled the lever that dropped the foot-rest down and brought the back upright, 'but I reckon Robert Prosky is happy to be doing his job, grateful even, I bet he's no trouble to no one. Doesn't give anybody any lip. Isn't an awld nuisance.' With that she reached down into her bag like she was looking for a mint or something. Now I think I said before that to my mind she allowed herself to be too influenced by the fillums and this proved to be her undoing. From out of her crammed bag she tried to draw a Beretta Mo. 92, 9mm semi-automatic pistol. A fine weapon in its way, used by every movie cop and the standard side arm of the US Army – but it isn't a quick draw weapon. Pistols are prone to jamming anyway and they've got all kinds of catches and clips and sights that can snag and hitch on stuff, as this one did on the string of the wrapper of a pack of adult incontinence pads. I on the other hand had chosen for my personal protection a revolver: Smith and Wesson short .38 police special, hammerless with the front sight ramped and filed down so there were no protrusions to stop me pulling it quick from the back of me pants. I was swinging the stubby barrel round on her, double handed, straight armed, when – realising she wasn't going to draw in time – she pulled the trigger and fired through the side of the bag. It was like a hot wind caught me, tossed me up and dropped me down behind the couch, chunks of which started to disappear, like a giant greedy bird was taking hungry pecks out of it. I couldn't hear a thing. I was deaf and my left shoulder was a pulp but I still rolled on to it bringing me into the middle of the room. Maureen put another one into my leg but, firing from the floor, I caught her once in the pelvis and again in the chest. She fell to her knees in front of me and I shot her again, twice in the head. I lay there for a bit then I reached up with me good arm and pressed the security bleeper round me neck. I could see the phone dialling itself.

I suppose they'll put me in prison . . . that shouldn't be so bad, harmless old bloke like me, I'll probably get a cushy job in the library or something. I might get myself a nice young lad as well, to be my girlfriend, do jobs for me and stuff. And if he gives me any trouble, I'll kill him.

YOU'RE ONLY
MIDDLE AGED ONCE

'No! Not you, no! Get out! You know you're barred, out!' This was the sort of thing Mike had had shouted at him quite a few times in pubs and bars but this was the first occasion it had been said in a hospital casualty department. 'This is a fucking hospital! You're supposed to treat everybody!' he shouted back at the nurse on the reception desk. 'Not you we're not,' she replied. 'We're supposed to treat sick people and you're not sick, you've never been sick. In fact you keep us from treating people who are sick. You're a fraud is what you are. And a nasty rude one at that. Now sod off!' Mike was inclined to stand there and argue but several alcoholics with terrible weeping head wounds began jeering at him so he turned and stomped out. He thought about trying another hospital but UCH was his local and he didn't really fancy travelling all the way to another casualty department. The fatigue that was an early symptom of the disease he was certain he suffered from had

83

become really intense, so he walked painfully and slowly back to his basement flat in Tavistock Place, wincing every few steps. He wondered the whole way how a nurse could be so nasty to someone clearly suffering from systemic lupus erythematosus. Occasionally he was so weak he had to clutch on to railings for support.

Mike had had what could reasonably be called a chequered career. Up at Oxford the same time as Mel and Angus and Rowan, he'd been on the edge of all that but had spent too much time on the dollies and the toot to really focus. Anyway, he was much brighter than those dimmocks. He could afford to pony around for a few years then at some point in the future he could zoom in on whatever he was going to do for the rest of his life, really concentrate, really fixate and then he'd be off up the road leaving all those other dummies to eat his exhaust smoke. Didn't really matter that he'd got sent down either, just meant more time to have fun. Five years in South America another two in LA, then back to Britain for the first of what turned out to be a string of knuckle-down times managing a middle-weight boxer who was going to be the new Sugar Ray Leonard, running a comedy club in Wolverhampton before it was fashionable, founding a restaurant serving Cajun cuisine in Manchester after it was fashionable, becoming a trader in hop futures, being the chief sales representative for the British made brand of Pomegranate personal computers and many more that he couldn't even remember and whose only memorial was in the dusty 'still pending' files of Interpol, the Forestry Commission and the Serious Fraud Office. Not the startlingly good career he'd imagined, but it did turn out that any fellow who'd been up at Oxford with Mel and Angus and Rowan would never want for a job in some sort of distant corner of the media. So in between his business ventures there were stints, like punctuation marks, writing training videos on the arcane twists and turns of Royal Mail package-sorting procedures, editing a comical Christmas book of recipes for cooking kittens, assistant producer of a radio wine quiz and so on. Now at the age of forty-two his main employment was a column in the Friday edition of a middle-brow tabloid newspaper that had seemed to be losing readers since its first day of publication in the early 1880s. His column was called 'You're Only Middle Aged Once' and at the top it featured a photograph of him looking what could only be described as 'roguish'. Its content was an often painful recounting of his life from day to day: the waking up, urine-soaked, in the alley behind a Soho drinking club, the multiple betrayals of women, the custody battles for children and motorbikes, in short the sort of stuff to be found somewhere in any mid- or up-market paper.

The only thing he had not shared with the readers was his hypochondria, though (in truth) it was his most constant companion. This fear of illness had stolen up on him suddenly when he was ten years old, a jolt, a childhood realisation that there were these things out there called diseases that could actually kill him. Him Mike, he could walk into a room where an illness was waiting and walk out carrying it and then a minute or a week or a year later there would be no more Mike. No Mike nowhere. You could look all over, under the bed, up the shelves, behind the box ottoman in the guest bedroom but there'd be no Mike anywhere because a disease had come and taken him away to nowhere. It was a thought that terrified him, though it also gave him a strange twist of contorted pleasure. From then on while other boys were going to the Saturday morning pictures or football practice, he was off down the doctor's, the casualty department or the library to hover over the medical dictionaries checking out his current imagined condition and picking up tips for what he could catch next.

Over the years the pattern would go like this: first there would be the spotting of the symptom, an abrupt noticing of a spot or a cough or a tremor that hadn't been there the day before. Then it generally needed only a microsecond to spin through the mental filing system and come up with the terrifying explanation: cancer!, cystic fybrosis!, multiple sclerosis!, dengue fever! Then there would be days of feverish thinking. The constant patrol for confirming signs like a tiny fort waiting for the dust storm of the approaching enemy column, the planning of the death-bed scene, the fevered imagining of his gradual decline. After that came the screwing up of courage for the visit to the hospital or the GP. Sometimes there would be a diagnosis right there, at other times a wait for test results. Either way there was always the reprieve, the statement that there was absolutely nothing wrong with him and what a rush that was! Better than any drug for it was literally the gift of life, a few words that told him that his existence was not over . . . yet.

The trip to the hospital that morning had been with what he thought were the first symptoms of a disease called lupus. But now he hadn't spoken to anybody, he hadn't got the rush, hadn't got the reprieve, it burned inside him like a rancid meal. It had to be got out somehow. Mike sat before his computer in the flat. On top of everything his column had to be in by the end of the afternoon and he couldn't think of anything to write about, he couldn't think of anything but his illness. After a few seconds he began to type.

'Lupus erythematosus is a chronic disease that causes inflammation of connective tissue, the material that sur-rounds body structures, bones and stuff and holds them together. It's an auto immune disorder in which the body's immune system for unknown reasons attacks the connective tissue as if it were foreign, causing inflammation. This morning at the hospital they told me I had it . . .' Eight hundred words spun out of him more easily than they ever had before, as he wrote about how he had first noticed the characteristic red, blotchy, almost butterfly-shaped rash over the cheeks and bridge of the nose. The feeling of fatigue, the loss of appetite, the fever, nausea, joint pain and the weight loss. Then he bravely recounted how he was sure that he didn't have the more serious and potentially fatal form systemic lupus erythematosus (SLE), which affects many systems of the body (as well as the skin) including the joints and the kidneys, but he promised to keep his readers informed. He smiled at the piece and then faxed it to the paper. He felt really calm, so calm that he felt able to open up the flight simulator on his computer and land a 747 at Singapore's Changi airport in a tropical rain storm.

His sub-editor rang about an hour later, 'Mike? Just got the column, bloody good bit of writing mate. But what exactly is all this about an illness?' Mike told him pretty much what he had written plus a few more details that he made up on the spot, all of it told in a weary but brave voice. The sub rang off wishing him good luck and when the column was printed he'd hardly mangled its punctuation or syntax at all.

Over the following week Mike got eight letters at the paper, three from lupus sufferers who said he would get better, one from a lupus sufferer who said he was going to die, one from a reader who said the disease was judgement from God for his sinful life, one from a single mother who said if he was ever in Basingstoke he should drop in, one saying he would be cured if only he took large doses of ginseng and one from a old man in Carlisle asking if there was anything he could do about his binmen.

Mike was surprised. He'd never had post before. His column had made an impact for the first time. Up until that point it had just been filling a hole in the paper, if he'd got fired (which he usually did) none of the readers would have noticed he'd gone, not until now anyway. He didn't want to push things though so the next week he wrote about a brawl he'd been involved in in the electrical goods department of John Lewis. After he'd faxed it off the sub-editor rang up. 'So the illness has gone away then has it?' he asked, to Mike's mind a tad suspiciously. 'No, not at all,' replied Mike, 'symptoms very severe in fact.' 'Well write about it then mate,' said the sub and rang off. So he did.

After a few weeks with an ever-growing post bag Mike was much more popular at work but his life improved in other ways too. The hypochondria that had been a loud voice yelling in his ear was still shouting but now it was from the far end of a long tunnel and so faint sometimes it could hardly be heard. And because his column had hinted at a greater mental seriousness that had come with the disease and because a man with lupus would hardly frequent Soho shebeens Mike was forced to stay away from his usual drinking clubs. He tried getting bugaluggs at home on a bottle of Asda own-brand vodka but he'd never liked solitary drinking so ended up sober for the first time in years. Weight loss was also a symptom he had cited in the paper so he spent some of the extra spare sober time he had doing press ups, sit ups and dancing around the flat to his old merengue records.

In his fifth post-illness column Mike wrote about how there was no known cure for lupus, how it is probable that the disease can be inherited and that hormonal factors play a part. Sometimes the agent that triggered the immune response (for example, a viral infection or sunlight) can be identified. The symptoms of both varieties of lupus periodically subside and recur with varying degrees of severity. SLE causes a variety of symptoms: there may be anaemia, neurological or psychiatric problems, kidney failure, pleurisy and pericarditis (inflammation of the membrane surrounding the heart). He did not yet know whether he had the serious variety or not but he was hopeful and calm.

By the end of the second month he was a hit at the paper with a whole heap of correspondence, he was fit, slim and in his first steady relationship for a long time and not with the usual media-nut-job either but a nice unmarried mother from Basingstoke. She was a woman he could show things to and teach things to. She'd never been to a Thai restaurant and it gave him a simple pleasure to see her take her first mouthful of tom yam gai. Before he'd met her he didn't know there was anybody left in Britain who hadn't been in one side of tom yam gai and out the other.

Round about week ten he sensed a certain slipping in the reader's voyeuristic interest in his illness so it was time to let slip that he was one of the 10 per cent of the people whose discoid lupus had evolved into the systemic form of the disease, which can affect almost any organ or system of the body. This cannot be predicted or prevented. Treatment of discoid lupus will not prevent its progression to the systemic form. Individuals who progress to the systemic form probably had systemic lupus at the outset, with the discoid rash as their main symptom. Systemic lupus is usually more severe than discoid lupus and can affect almost any organ or system of the body. For some people, only the skin and joints will be involved. In others, the joints, lungs, kidneys, blood or other organs and/or tissues may be affected. There was an immediate uprush of interest and the woman from Basingstoke allowed him to sodomise her for the first time.

Mike did sense, however, that there was a finite limit to the value of his recounting of the progress of the disease no matter how stoic his endurance. So while he was having a skin biopsy to look for specific antibodies that are directed against the body's own tissues, he introduced his readers to Dr Samir Naryahan a tall, dark-haired refugee from the Lebanon. He talked of Dr Sammy's dark sardonic humour, the long hours he worked, the dark circles under his eyes, the crummy hospital-owned bedsit he lived in. The country fell in love with Dr Sammy and if they loved the saturnine dermatologist then their hearts absolutely burst for little Laura Loxton . . . Mike first met this brave little tyke when she happened to have the appointment before him at the clinic. The stories he told of her stoicism in the face of such terrible suffering set such an example of simple-hearted infant courage that the public's interest became positively fevered. If Laura had existed and gone out into the street for a little walk she would have been torn to bits by people who wanted to shower her with their undiluted love. They would say to their own children, 'Darren you fucking bastard! Why can't you be more like little Laura Loxton?' Soon Laura became too popular and despite Mike's pleas to respect the family's fragile privacy, the tabloid newspapers began to hunt for little Laura. Little Laura succumbed to kidney failure with astonishing rapidity and departed this world leaving Mike's readers with the thought, encapsulated in her last words, 'Live every day like you're in Tenerife.' Many wept openly at the news of little Laura's demise, including several mothers and fathers who had not cried when their own children had died.

To counter the traumatic loss of little Laura, Mike introduced Nurse Jayne Corcoran from Lincoln. As blonde as Dr Sammy was dark, at first they didn't take to each other but it was not long before Mike was hinting that there was some sexual healing going on between these two. Both were damaged people in their own way and who amongst us would begrudge them the consolation they found in each other's embrace. Though Mike did get a couple of letters at the paper complaining about Nurse Corcoran's blonde purity being violated by 'a coon'.

This was one of Mike's good times too. The lupus was in remission. Nevertheless, come the winter and there was what the medics called 'a flare' in his affliction. Mike was sorry to tell his readers of the sudden explosion of symptoms, achy joints, the fever over a hundred degrees, prolonged and extreme fatigue, arthritis, skin rashes, anaemia and Raynaud's phenomenon in which his fingers turned blue in the cold. A cloud also settled over the love of Dr Sammy and Nurse Corcoran when he was seen by a rather nasty radiographer call Maxitone in a wine bar called the Bottle Green Bowler Hat, kissing and cuddling with a dark-haired woman, possibly called Shakira or Shamura. 'Just what you'd expect from a wog,' as the racist letter writer put it.

Mike told the readers that he might have been censorious towards Dr Sammy before the onset of his flare, but now, though his swollen fingers could hardly type, he reminded everyone who read his column to 'Live every day like you're in Tenerife.' Who were we, he asked, to judge a man such as Dr Samir Naryahan, a man who had seen so much pain, had helped so many but was constantly reminded of the limits of even his mighty powers. In her sensible Fenland's way, Nurse Corcoran felt the same, she knew Dr Sammy would return to her when he had tired of this Levantine temptress. The woman in Basingstoke also forgave Mike for fucking a British Midland's stewardess in Glasgow while he was at a book signing though she wouldn't let him bugger her any more.

In January Mike was voted Columnist of the Year and his book *Shadow of the Wolf* a collection of his pieces for the paper, was at number one in the paperback charts. Mike managed to attend the awards dinner and pick up his prize even though he was on non-steroidal anti-inflammatory drugs to relieve the joint pain, antimalarial drugs for the skin rash, corticosteroid drugs for fever, pleurisy and neurological symptoms and cytoxi immunosuppressant drugs for the kidney damage. He got a standing ovation from the usually cynical journalists, many of whom wept as he painfully approached the podium. They were glad to see that one of their own derided profession could show such quiet gutsiness in the face of that amount of pain. It made them feel better about themselves and the terrible things they did.

The morning after the dinner Mike noticed a lacy membrane covering the inside of his cheeks, some soreness on his gums and some small blister-like swellings on the lining of his lips. He was so unconcerned that he didn't look up these symptoms in his extensive collection of medical encyclopædias. The most likely explanation was either oral thrush or a mild auto immune condition called lichen planus, certainly nothing to worry about but he thought he should get it checked out. He decided to visit the casualty department of an out-of-the-way hospital in south-east London he had sometimes used in the old days when he'd visited UCH too many times in a week.

He gave a false name to the receptionist and waited. A young South African doctor whose name tag read Dr Rod Melon came quite rapidly and took him into a side examination room. He studied Mike's mouth for some considerable time prodding around with a torch, then he sighed and slowly put his torch away. 'I think you should sit down Mr Waugh,' he said. Mike slowly sank into a chair feeling uneasy. 'Why, what's up?' he quavered. 'Surely it's only oral thrush or lichen planus, isn't it?'

'I'm afraid not,' replied Dr Melon in a serious voice. 'They are superficially similar. Nevertheless what you have is Harper's Syndrome. It is not well known in this country but is more common in Africa. I'm very sorry to say it is a condition of the auto immune system that is rapid, fatal and untreatable.'

Mike left the hospital and walked home even though it was over five miles. Where the road bent he often walked straight on, going in the front doors of buildings and coming out of the back or through the window, or in one case smashing down a flimsy dividing wall. When he got down to his basement flat he sat staring at the carpet until it got dark. Finally, he stirred himself with a shudder and went into the bathroom. From the cabinet he took out a bottle of thirty Ativan tranquillisers he had left over from his hypochondriac days. With a glass of tap water he took them one by one then lay down to die.

Back at the hospital Rod saw a couple more patients then he carefully removed the name tag he'd made on his home computer and put it in his trouser pocket. He took off the white coat, put it back in the cupboard where he'd found it and strolled outside to his pizza delivery bike: time to get on with his real job. He smiled happily to himself about the good afternoon he'd had, that was his favourite thing telling the ones who had nothing wrong with them that they were seriously ill and the ones who were critical that they were unequivocally fine. It was brilliant pretending to be a doctor, much better than going to all the trouble of learning to be a real one.

NIC AND TOB

Nic and Tob were a double act. They say a double act is like a marriage. I suppose this is true if both people in the marriage are men and appear on television talking nonsense. This apparently genial pair of rubbish-talking Northerners had been around for about ten years. And they'd been a good ten years. Their arrival on the comedy scene had fortunately coincided with the rise of stupidity, the public having tired of being shouted at by fat men about things that weren't their fault as a form of light entertainment. The public were ready for an easy ride and Nic and Tob were never going to rock the stage coach; they were happy to provide the easiest of undemanding rides. Recently though, Nic, a self-obsessed neurotic underneath his velvet suit, had been in the BBC TV club bar after a recording of one of their undemanding quiz shows and overheard one BBC top executive, waiting to get served, say to another top executive, 'You know I've been thinking that maybe we should do more than pander to the lowest taste of the idiot public, chasing every will o' the wisp, voguish fad. Perhaps as a public broadcast organisation we should try to illuminate the world with a bright pure light of elevating joy.' (As it turned out this man had been in the middle of a nervous breakdown and was soon fired, later becoming an organic baker in Penrith.) But Nic was not to know this and he panicked. Comedians are skittish creatures at the best of times, the mink of the showbusiness world – nice coats but snickering and sniffing the air, chittering and weaving sinuously through the undergrowth, biting those that try to pet them and wiping out any rival wildlife that comes their way. He called a meeting with Tob to discuss what they could do if stupid went out of the window. What they needed they concluded was an edge, an edge that would fireproof them against any swing in fashion.

It is one of the perils of cable television these days that viewers pick up a lot more half-baked or half-defrosted ideas off programmes on the Discovery Channel. Tob had half-watched a film about Caribbean witchcraft on his giant flatscreen a few days before. It was he who came up with the idea that they should become practitioners of Santaria, obeah or, as it is most commonly known, voodoo. He thought it could really help their careers if they became disciples of Baron Samedi. After all, say what you like about the supposed benefits of High Church Anglicanism, chi gong or sacred cranial massage none of them offers the promise of raising the dead to do your bidding.

Fired up with enthusiasm they set their personal assistant

the simple task of finding the best teacher of voodoo that there was to be had in all of Britain and get him or her to come to their house for voodoo lessons, just like they had when they were going through their karate phase. They thought it would be easy: after all she had found them their personal trainers, found them a really good drug dealer and found a fiancée for Tob. The best voodoo teacher couldn't be that hard. You might ask, 'Couldn't they find a teacher for themselves?' No way José. In the same way that it takes five pay clerks, engineers and cooks to put one infantryman into the front line, so it takes a monstrous regiment of drivers, agents, lawyers and PAs to get one comedian to the battlefront of comedy, each of them submerging their ego, giving a piece of it to the star they service so that they grow huge and glow like the sun.

It came as a shock to all concerned then that, no matter how much money they were offered, there was nobody who would teach the lads the ins and outs of voodoo. Everywhere their PA went she was given the same nonsense about this knowledge being so potent it had to be earned, had to be suffered for, couldn't just be taught to any glib white man who wanted a superficial, Reader's Digest version of an ancient art. This wasn't t'ai chi you know.

There was nothing for it – they would have to go to Haiti, the home of vodun. People there were poorer and, as is always the way, scruples counted for less. At least the trip would be tax deductible. Their PA found a contact in Haiti who was more used to facilitating European couples who wanted to adopt little black babies but who was happy to hook two middle-aged men up with a voodoo houngan, a priest of that ancient religion brought many centuries ago by Yoruba slaves to the terrible isle of Haiti.

Now you would think highly paid celebrities like Nic and Tob would spend their money freely, ensuring only the best for themselves, but – perhaps because they get so much stuff for free – when they're spending their own cash they can be remarkably cheesy. So it was a mini-cab that picked them up in turn from their side by side Kent mansions. They liked to use a firm called Only Airports, late-model Scorpios and Omegas driven by sleep-deprived Nigerian religious maniacs, only twenty-five quid and get you to Gatwick in under thirty-five minutes, rush hour or no.

They don't talk much on the trip to the airport. They'd been on the piss the night before with Mark Lamarr in the Groucho Club so there are thumping hangovers to contend with but in reality it's more that the lads don't really like each other much any more. They've only bought economy tickets on the Virgin plane but their agent's phoned ahead and they easily get bumped up to the wide, padded seats of Upper Class. They like that the boys do, it makes them happy. A few glasses of champagne before take-off and they are revving again like the engines of the 747. At Miami International there's a two hour layover before taking a smaller propeller plane to the airport at Port-au-Prince. Luckily, Nic and Tob are recognised by a group of British accountants on their way to a conference in Baton Rouge so they join them at the bar for a drink and hold them enthralled with silliness and stories of life inside the television. They love that the boys do.

In January 1998 the US Secretary of Transportation determined that Port-au-Prince international airport did not maintain and carry out effective safety or security measures. Therefore it was a ratty little twenty seater private plane that flew the boys to Haiti, a tiny flying shoebox that was as full as full can be with fat black women, 'higglers', they were called. They bought whatever was in demand back on the island at the malls of Miami, trying unsuccesfully to haggle with the staff at K-mart, and shipped it as hand luggage to be sold in the street markets of Port-au-Prince. A more planned economy might have cut out the fat women and just shipped the stuff as cargo or at the very least sent some thin women who would have weighed the plane down less, but that was another measure of Haiti's desperate straits. So with a mammy jamming Nic and Tob up against the window, they limped their way across the cobalt Caribbean till they plunged vertiginously to the airport at Port-au-Prince. It took two hours to collect the half of their luggage they could find. Sweating and tired they lugged their bags into the arrivals hall. The flight destination boards set high into the walls of the airport had long ago given up the ghost, their letters frozen now in a rictus of nonsense. The boys looked up and read 'Flight gahnagg. Via erghhhhh. Destination Aaaaghhh'. Nic and Tob felt they had landed at Aaaaghhh and what was worse they had booked to stay there for three whole weeks.

Mr René Monuma their contact, the baby man, himself looking like a fat sweating baby, grabbed them up from the arrivals hall just as some beggars were sticking their stumps in the boys' faces. Apologising profusely he bundled them into his old Peugeot that stood ticking at the kerb. 'Forgive me gentlemen, for my tardiness, army checkpoints I am afraid.' He took a huge nickel-plated Colt Python .45 revolver out of his back pocket and sat on it before putting the car in gear, shouting, 'Lock the doors please!' and ploughing into the crowds that churned across the road. They bounced over huge potholes in the road, past great piles of rotting garbage. Whenever they were forced to stop, various people tried to climb into the car but Mr Monuma deterred them with a string of swearing in Creole and a wave of the Colt. They swerved up unlit roads until the car swung through a battered pair of gates guarded by a ragged black man, a gleaming, meticulously oiled, twelve-gauge, pump-action shotgun dangling from his hands. This was to be the boys' hotel, the very one that Graham Greene modelled the Hotel Trianon on in *The Comedians*. The boys would have known that if they had ever read a book, but they hadn't. Tob had once, remarkably, got a question on *University Challenge* right but only because he was the answer.

All of the next day Nic and Tob stayed in the hotel compound. It was only once night closed in that Mr Monuma returned to take them up into the hills for their first free introductory lesson at the newly founded International University of Voodoo (formerly the Polytechnic of Voodoo). First of all, an introductory meal in the canteen: deep-fried malanga (a root vegetable with spices) and griot-fried pork, plus a voucher entitling them to a free cocktail. Then it was classes, classes, classes. Over the following three weeks they attended lectures split into history, theory and practice. They learnt of the roots of vodun or Sevi Lwa, the creation of the West African Yoruba people occupying eighteenth- and nineteenth-century Dahomey; they were told of the loas, the vodun deities and they learnt some of their names: Samedi the god of the cemetery, Sousson Pannan an ugly loa covered with sores, totally evil, with a taste for drinking spirits and blood. They learnt many voodoo rituals and their purpose, which is to make contact with these loa. Night after dark night they attended the university's own hounfour, the voodoo temple, where they sat hour after hour before the poteau-mitan, the pole where the gods communicate with the people. There were long lessons in altar making, elaborately decorating it with candles, pictures of Christian saints, symbolic items related to the spirits and so on. They learnt that the most important components of humans are the two parts of the soul, the ti-bon-ange and the gros-bon-ange, which means, literally, 'great good angel'. Nic and Tob were told that at the time of conception, part of the cosmic lifeforce passes into the human being. This is the force that all living

things share, connecting us to each other in a great web
of energy. The gros-bon-ange keeps the body alive and
sentient and after death passes back into the reservoir of
energy in the cosmos. Without the gros-bon-ange, a person
loses their lifeforce. It is possible, according to vodun belief,
to separate a person's gros-bon-ange from him or her and
store it in a bottle or jar, where the energy can be directed
to other purposes. The other half of a person's soul is the
ti-bon-ange, meaning 'little good angel', which is the source
of personality. The ti-bon-ange represents the accumulation
of a person's knowledge and experience and is responsible
for determining individual characteristics, personality and
will. It can leave the body, when dreaming for instance or
when the body is being possessed by a loa. The ti-bon-ange
is the part of the human make-up that is most vulnerable
to sorcery, even more so than the gros-bon-ange. And they
were taught the ins and outs of the angajan, the pact between
the loa and a person involving malevolent magic. Certain
loa are partners in black magic and will perform harmful
services in exchange for a great sacrifice of some sort (or
the down payment on a Yamaha jet ski).

By the middle of the third week there was a graduation
ceremony where the boys were officially made bokors, fully
initiated priests of vodun, albeit ones who perform black
magic. Another name for bokors is 'those who serve the
loa with both hands'. Nic and Tob were ready to do that.

When they got back to England the boys were keen to
make a start but they had to wait for nearly a week till

DHL delivered their half-container load of ingredients from Haiti. They started out small: 'Let's shrivel Jim Davidson's dick,' was one of Tob's first suggestions. They brought that about in their bagi, their room containing an altar dedicated to the loa.

Then it was time to set about using the magic they had learnt to help their careers. One of the teachers had told them that during the period in which the ti-bon-ange hovers over the body after death, a bokor can capture it and turn it into a zombie astral. Unlike a zombie, which is a dead body without a soul, a zombie astral is a dead soul without a body. It wanders around and performs deeds at the command of the bokor, never allowed to achieve a final rest. The boys wondered whether it was possible to capture the ti-bon-ange of a computer so they hid in the offices of the Light Entertainment department of the BBC until a temp switched off her PC and left the room, then they threw rum and three pennies on it and beat it with a calabash stick. Sure enough all the computers in the corporation were now their zombie astrals. Right away they got the machines to give approval and a huge budget to the sitcom that they were planning to write about a family of oysters who lived off the coast of Kent.

What took up most of the boys' time though was the creation of zombies. What would happen was that the pair would perform a ritual that causes a targeted person to die and, within a certain amount of time, they would then call them back to life, now as a body without its soul. They would raise the victim after a day or two and administer a hallucinogenic concoction called the 'zombies cucumber' that revived the victim. Once the zombie was revived, it had no power of speech, and its senses were dulled. The human personality is entirely absent, and the memory is gone. Zombies were thus easy to control. Soon Nic and Tob had taken control of the souls of so many people in the media that the private clubs of Soho were swamped with white-faced, drooling, emotionally-dead-inside, palpably decaying crowds. Through the use of spells they had also enslaved in love six women and two men and obtained a 25 per cent discount at any World of Leather store in the South-east of England.

After some six months the boys were ready for their most complex enterprise yet. Obtaining the spirits of six dead people from the cemetery in a ceremony called prise du mort and invoking the loa of the cemetery, Baron Cimetière, they sent them out to infect the minds of the jury judging prizes for that year's BAFTA awards in light entertainment. They were after a record-breaking twenty-six nominations. But it didn't work. Sure, one of the judges threw himself out of the window and another became convinced that she was a cornish pasty and tried to microwave herself, but none of them voted for Nic and Tob. The boys were devastated. Their spell hadn't worked and they didn't know why.

They didn't know why. I know why. Don't laugh when I tell you this but the finest cuisine to be had in all of Europe, perhaps in the whole world, can be found in Austria. See you're laughing but it's true. You think Austrian food is too heavy, too stodgy, too bland. Which it is ... here. Say you want to cook some Austrian classic here in Britain. So you buy the finest ingredients and follow a recipe given to you by Herbert Berger, native of Innsbruck and Michelin-starred chef. Or you go further. You can fly in Salzburg's top chef to cook it for you. And it still comes out tasting like that stuff your stereo comes packed in. But eat the same dish, cooked the same way in Vienna and it is stupendous. Why the difference? There are a few cuisines that are robust enough to travel: Italian, Chinese, French cooking can all be eaten anywhere in the world, can take the substitution of local ingredients and still remain true to themselves; but many others — Austrian, Russian, Spanish for example — simply do not work outside their own borders. There is some connection between the climate and the produce and the way the produce is cooked that breaks down once the cooking goes abroad. The same is true of magic. There are some magics that will work as reliably all over the world as a Zippo lighter — voodoo is not one of these. For voodoo to be consistently effective it needs to feed on the humid air of the Caribbean, it needs an atmosphere dripping with the quavering thoughts of a million terrified believers, the powders, bones, herbs, must soak in the soil where Baron Samedi still watches over the graveyard and the rada drums still echo over the denuded hills. Take them from that air, that atmosphere, that soil and they begin to shed their power or take on strange new capacity. Either way they can no longer be bid.

Though they tried over and over again, the results were not there. Nic and Tob were devastated to see their power go, they wept and tried to cast one last big spell, a spell that would earn them so much money that they would at least be able to live in comfort for the rest of their lives and wreak revenge on a detested enemy.

They boys wanted to raise a duppy, which is an evil spirit. Some sects of vodun believe that everyone has evil in them; while the soul, called in this case the duppy, is in the body, it is controlled by the heart and brain, and a person will not abandon himself or herself to evil. Once the duppy is released in death, however, it no longer has this restraint and is capable of terrible acts. Nic and Tob wanted their duppy to terrorise the Manchester United goalkeeper during a, whoever was sponsoring it that year, second round tie of the League Cup, against their beloved Doncaster Rovers. The two men bet all the money they could raise on a surprise win for the Rovers, then they set about bringing it about. The pair were meticulous when casting the veve and used the finest farine: cornmeal flown from Haiti the night before in the diplomatic bag of the Dominican Embassy, they followed every twist and turn of the spell to raise the duppy: late into the night the rada drums beat out over the Kent countryside.

Expectantly, the boys settled down in front of Sky Sport at Nic's house, chugged a few beers and saw their team stuffed six nil. After the game had finished, letters in blood, five foot high appeared on Nic's living room wall, dripping on to the carpet and spelling out the message:

NIC AND TOB DON'T TRY TO FUCK WITH THE UNITED! ALL THE BEST, CHEERS, SIR ALEX. PS NEW ALTERNATIVE AWAY STRIP COMING SOON, ORDER NOW FOR SPECIAL DISCOUNT. PPS LOVED THE SHOW ABOUT OYSTERS.

BIG-HEADED CARTOON ANIMAL

'I haven't had one of these all year and now I get two in the same day. Other was a German guy this mornin',' said the very fat woman behind the immigration desk at Los Angeles International Airport. The 'one of these' to which she referred was a code added to the visa waiver in Pete's British passport: 212 (d) (3) (A) (28). This code when tapped into the computer of the feared 'La Migra' – the illegal Hispanic's word for the dreaded Immigration Department – would kick out the information that Pete and the German guy had both answered 'yes' to the question 'Are you now or have you ever been a member of a Communist organisation?' on their visa application forms. Pete imagined the German was some ex-Baader Meinhof member now on his way to take extensive meetings trying to raise finance for some Euro pudding movie who would be back by the end of the week feeling sorry that he'd given up terrorism and wondering what the price was for a used Heckler and

Koch 9mm and some Semtex only slightly past its sell-by date. Pete had thought about lying when he'd come to the question but there was probably a file about him somewhere and he was proud of his past anyway so didn't feel that it was something to be denied. That wasn't the main reason though – above all he felt it was simply wrong to fill in a government form incorrectly. Gustave Flaubert once wrote, 'Inside every revolutionary there is a policeman', and inside every ex-revolutionary there is a man who works in an insurance office in Hastings.

Mind you Pete hadn't fled as far from his younger, more principled self as some ex-comrades had, indeed he felt himself to be still very much in the game of world improvement. His job was deputy director of a London based charity called Libertad which concerned itself with the care and resettlement of victims of torture and imprisonment from all over Latin America. It was a very good cause and like all organisations whose sole purpose was trying to do undiluted good Libertad was torn with the most violent internal feuds, bitter, poisonous rivalries and corrosive, internecine hatreds. Pete sometimes wondered if in organisations devoted solely to the spread of terrible evil: the Waffen SS say, or the Ukrainian Mafia or the Bosch Domestic Appliances Repairs Department, if there wasn't within these groups an atmosphere of mutual loving support within the boundaries of a caring, sharing environment. There was probably nothing one Serb sniper wouldn't do for another Serb sniper, they probably spent a lot of time in the trenches donating sperm and kidneys to each other and letting their wives use their wombs for surrogate children.

There was none of that in Libertad; it was more than your cojones were worth to ask somebody to pass you a pencil. In Libertad, amongst others there was the feud between the volunteers and the full-time staff and there was the feud between the lesbians with the full cavalry moustaches and the lesbians with the lipstick, high heels and the leather micro skirts. The biggest feud though, the biggest gulf, was between the tortured and the untortured. It was in truth a very one-sided feud since the tortured (all of them of course Latin Americans) occupied the moral heights, impregnably sandbagged by the fact of their past anguish. The South Americans who had been imprisoned and tortured wore their suffering like a laminated security pass giving them access to all areas. Pete couldn't believe how sanctimonious somebody could be just because they'd once had a soldering iron stuck up their arse. Pete was stuck on his career path and was bitter about it, he was forty-five and should have been director of his own charity by now but it would be impossible for him to rise any further in Libertad without him being tortured and there wasn't much chance of that. Bloody wishy-washy British Government, you couldn't even rely on them to organise a proper death squad, unless you were Irish perhaps. Indeed Pete thought he'd managed to be as persecuted for his political beliefs as it was possible to be in Britain. Think about it, he was suffering now. After all, if he hadn't once been in the Communist Party and dedicated his student years to the struggling masses of the world then he wouldn't now be being held up at immigration by a two hundred ton woman. Just then, however, she waved him through with a cheery, 'Enjoy your holiday in America,' and he was on the official soil of the United States a lot faster than many people who hadn't once plotted to put its thirty-sixth and thirty-seventh presidents on trial for 'war crimes against the people of Laos and Cambodia'.

His partner Pru came through soon after, they collected their luggage and got a cab. Pete directed the swarthy moustachioed driver, in his slow Spanish, to take them to the Ma Maison Hotel on La Cienaga Boulevard opposite the famous Beverley Center. The driver complied even though he was Iranian, '*Valle! De acuerdo companeros,*' he said to his fares and took them there the very long way round. All the way the cabbie eyed Pru in the rear-view mirror, she was a fine-looking woman. Pete and Pru had met at a Labour Party meeting in the early 1980s and they made a good team: Pru was the director of an animal rights charity and the internal warfare in that organisation made Libertad, look very tame indeed.

It had been her idea to come to the States for their holiday. Pete had wanted to go as they usually did to France: there was a village near Perpignan that was more than half occupied by ex-Hackney Council employees. These people had given each other hugely generous retirement pensions and munificent redundancy pay-offs then decamped to France, putting as much distance between themselves and Hackney as it was possible to, while still being able to pick up Radio 4 on Long Wave. For the poor remaining French in the village it was a second occupation and on balance they would rather have had the Werhmacht back. They hid politically incorrect tins of foie gras and copies of *Penthouse* in much the same way as their grandparents had hidden radio transmitters and Sten guns. Pete and Pru usually went there, passing from one restored barn to another but this year Pru had said she was fucking sick of it and wanted to go to America instead. Pete was shocked at first. He had of course been to Guatemala, Venezuela and Chile but he had never even thought of visiting the hated 'El Norte', the toad that squatted in the North, sucking up people and resources that never came back to the poor South.

Pru said she wanted air conditioning and power showers and swimming pools and huge quantities of bland foods and stuff at The Gap that cost the same in dollars as it cost in pounds in Upper Street Islington. So Pete got the tube in his lunch hour down to the same embassy in Grosvenor Square that he had thrown rocks at in the 1960s and filled in his application for a visa waiver.

Now, they were in the United States. And not just the United States, but the Unitedest State of them all, California: Los Angeles, California. They fell in love with the place straight away. For a start everybody was so good-looking; the most beautiful people in the world had been coming here for nearly a century and mating with each other so it was no surprise when you thought about it and you got the feeling

119

that ugly people were stopped at the LA county line. Pete and Pru were good-looking too and they had had no idea how great it would be to be amongst like-faced individuals. One day while they were having lunch at the Beverley Center Pete saw a group of obviously just arrived British tourists. It was like there'd been a nuclear war back home while they were on their holidays that the parochial US news hadn't mentioned and these were the resulting mutants: snaggle-toothed, curved-spined homunculi that staggered about, dribble spooling from their mouths, their knuckles brushing along the ground.

There was even a look that Peter and Pru would give to other good-looking couples, a drooped eyelid, slight nod that said 'we're lovely, you're lovely, ain't it great?'. It was almost a religious experience; Pete thought this must be how a Jew felt visiting Israel for the first time, seeing Jews here, Jews there, Jews every fucking where. And the similarity went further because the supporting role of the Palestinians whose land it had once been was played here in Los Angeles by the People of Mexico. Everywhere they went small brown people would scuttle out to take their car, take their coat, clip their nearby rose bushes. Do whatever, more or less whenever. One day driving down the brown, semi-dangerous end of Sunset Boulevard they saw a sad, huddled group of Latinos waiting on a corner for fat gringos to come by in pick-ups offering casual work under a dripping angry graffiti that read 'DON'T HIRE THESE SCUM!' 'But if they didn't,' thought Peter 'who'd do all the work?'

By and large they did not do the obvious sights, preferring the Watts Towers in the South Central hood to the Museum of Modern Art, the office block in Century City where Bruce Willis iced the terrorists in the first and best *Die Hard* movie, to the *Queen Mary* and the Spruce Goose at Long Beach. Nevertheless, towards the end of their two weeks there was nothing for it: it was time to visit the theme park. The original theme park, the magic kingdom, supposedly the happiest place in the fucking world.

So early one morning they climbed into their swishy, swoopy Oldsmobile Rocket 88 and took the Santa Anna Freeway to Anaheim. They got there before the place opened and therefore got a good parking place near the entrance. When the gates swung open they were among the first on to Main Street USA. The park was waiting for them, cleaner than an operating theatre, candy-spun buildings twinkling in the spring sunlight, little tractor trains poop, pooping their whistles ready to welcome on board the first passengers of the day. And the place was already thronged with employees, vendors in Barbershop outfits, jazz bands and blazered security people whose smiling eyes twitched this way and that and who were either connected to some central control by tiny ear pieces or the theme park had filled their entire disabled quota by farming out their security to the Deaf Association of America. Most of all though there were the big-headed cartoon animals: employees dressed in costumes with the big painted fibreglass heads of the famous animated characters. There was the mouse, there was the

121

mouse's girlfriend, there was the dog, the duck was there, the thing that looked like a dog, but couldn't be because it owned the dog, was there, plus loads of the more modern characters that Pete didn't know because he didn't have any children and hadn't seen any of the films since 1978. They were already into their daily business of bothering people, the big-headed cartoon animals, waving their big silly feet, clocking children on the heads with their big clumsy hands, waddling about, marching in the early morning parade. Capering and dancing and getting their photos took.

One of them seemed to want to be Pete's friend. He came over to Pete in a rush, trying to clasp at him with its big fibreglass paddles. It was the dog that wasn't a dog and it seemed to be trying to tell him something but all that came out of its mouth was a muffled mumbling from way down inside its head, like the sound of a throat-cancer patient shouting from the bottom of a very deep well. Pete found its desperate embrace repulsive and easily pushing it off he caught up with Pru. Pete sneaked a quick look back, it was staring forlornly after him, its big mutant hands hanging by its side. 'Get a grip for fuck's sake mate, don't take the job so serious.'

Pru was heading straight for the rides, she wanted to go on the rides very much and Pete wanted to go on the rides too. After only a short wait of about thirty minutes they were strapped into the ride that was supposed to be like a trip through the asteroid belt and for the next three minutes Pete was in what he felt after was an extended high-speed car crash with giant biscuits flying at him. He would have vomited if the G force hadn't kept every ounce of bile crammed down his throat. 'Whoo, wasn't that fantastic?' said Pru when they tumbled off. 'I am never ever going on one of those fucking things ever again,' said Pete, then sat down straight on his backside, his legs no longer up to the job of supporting him.

They agreed that Pru would go on the rides and Pete would keep himself amused with all the other stuff, then they would meet up in the early evening for the electric parade that came down main street at sundown. Everybody said you had to see that. So Pete had all day to wander the park and look around. This was not something that often happened – an inquisitive bored man who had the time to look closely at the park. As he wandered, sometimes he would catch a glimpse of Pru, she would go shooting past in a log hurtling over a waterfall or he would see her on the horizon, a screaming passenger on a runaway train. He mooched and as he mooched he got bored and fractious. He had plenty of time for reflection and reflection is a bad, dangerous thing in a theme park: you notice things.

The first thing he noticed was that if they were kept out of Hollywood then this was where they let all the ugly folk come. Pete and Pru's window cleaner had once told them about a visit he'd taken with his wife and kids to the other, bigger theme park in Florida. They'd become obsessed about the huge number of gigantic, enormous-arsed, fat people who were bump-bumping about the place. Every time they spotted one of these blimp people one of the kids would shout 'Hot dog!' then go and stand in front of the fat people, as if posing for a photo. When they got home their snaps were entirely of huge fat persons with their children in front of them. Hot dogs.

Pete felt it was like being in the middle of a parade of inflatable figures, the number of hot dogs that were around him. Secondly, he noticed the undeclared guerrilla war (rather like the one in Guatemala) that was going on between the children and the big-headed cartoon animals. The groins of the costumed figures seemed to present an irresistible temptation for the kids; every few minutes he would see a tot reach out and grab the balls of the duck or the dog or the mouse. The only weapons the animals had in their armoury were the sly elbow to the stomach or the seemingly accidental slash of beak to the head when nobody was looking. These weapons were deployed as often as possible but it seemed that the cartoon creatures were still getting the worst of it. Occasionally, Pete would see off in the distance the dog that wasn't a dog, which seemed to want to talk to him, but he didn't have any difficulty getting away from it: after all it's not possible to travel very fast when your shoes are four feet long.

What came to obsess Pete over the day, just as the fat folk had obsessed his window cleaner, was how clean the place was and where all the rubbish went. These thousands of tourists, especially the fat ones, generated billions of tons of crap every second as far as Pete could see but he couldn't tell where any of it was going. They would stuff their junk into the hundreds of bins and the bins would gratefully take their junk but nobody ever came to empty them. Taking his lunch in one of the many terrible food outlets he also saw that there was no 'backstage' to the place, there was no rear to the building, it was all highly profitable serving space – unlike the usual fast food outlet there were no greasy crash doors with piles of garbage and trays of deliveries leaning against them, it was all front. The stuff must be coming and going some other way. Pete bought a milkshake and going closer to a bin dropped it in. He listened to hear it drop on to the pile of taco wrappers that a nearby herd of grazing fattybores had stuffed into it seconds earlier but he didn't hear it hit at all, it just seemed to vanish with no sound. Going round the back of the bin he saw that it could be pivoted via a hinge set into its concrete base, returning to the front he found a small catch that he hadn't noticed at first. He clicked the catch upwards and with a hiss the bin tipped backwards until it lay flat on the ground revealing a circular shaft, its walls lined with the slime of a trillion junk meals dropping perhaps fifty feet into Stygian darkness. Pete stuck his head down the shaft to see where it ended and just at that moment one of the Ugly Family Robinson who had been munching nearby stepped back to try and get a shot on his video cam of his entire family, though in truth he would have had to step into the next state to fit them all in. Retreating like a reversing hippopotamus one of his giant buttocks brushed Pete whose head was down the hole and the force was enough to pitch him down it with a startled cry. Such was the vast distance between the arse of the fat man and his brain that no neural messages had got through from that region in many years, it was a lost continent of lard to which doomed cerebral stimuli, like relief columns to a blubber Stalingrad, were sent never to return. He never knew what he had done.

Pete hurtled down the grease-slick shaft expecting at any second the smack of concrete that would break his bones, but instead he bounced to a landing on a huge pile of hamburger cartons and half-eaten burritos. Looking up he saw the circle of light that illuminated his landing spot disappear as the bin hissed automatically back into its original position. He didn't have long to consider his position before the rubbish pile started moving. With a jerk it began to trundle down a long tunnel lit by harsh neon lights set into the roof. Raising his head over the lip of the wagon Pete saw that he was in the last of a train of rubbish skips, similar to the coal wagons in a mine that carry the coal to the mine head, swaying along on narrow rails and pulled by a locomotive bellowing black diesel fumes into the confined tunnel. At the controls of the loco was a Mexican woman, her clothes were faded and patched, a mournful, hungry expression on her face. Something wrong here. The stink of diesel went some way but only some to masking the appalling stench of decay and rot that was all around, it made him almost want to gag for the second time that day. Maybe, he thought, this was some strange kind of ride. The smelliest place on earth.

The rubbish train entered a larger tunnel, tracks running

either side of it like tributaries joining a mighty river, trains empty and overflowing with waste going this way and that, at the wheels of each a sad faced Hispanic. After a while they passed through a sort of station with stairs perhaps leading upwards, almost certainly back to the surface but guarding the platform was a large blond man in the theme park uniform, earpiece in place, a pump-action shotgun balanced on his hip, and somehow it did not seem a good place to get off the train. Then an amazing sight, out of the tunnel and into a huge domed hall, St Paul's Cathedral fitted out by Piranesi, lined with gigantic bellowing furnaces their cast-iron funnels spiralling into the apex of the dome, the heat from the furnaces fed into boilers, the boilers driving belts and chains and pistons, the belts and chains and pistons disappearing into the roof and powering the rides above and out of sight, though dimly heard. The open maws of the furnaces fed by hundreds of sweating Hispanics shovelling in the litter that the trains tipped from their wagons. And all around on gantries armed guards, tall and Nordic for the most part, in contrast to those slaving below.

In the days before CCTV cameras Pete might have stood a chance but not now. As soon as the train stopped strong arms hauled him out of the wagon, four guards marched him out of the dome down long corridors to a sort of underground police station, presumably the headquarters of the park's security forces. He was taken into a room, an interview room familiar from a thousand copshows. An older man came in after a while and asked Pete what he was doing there and Pete told him, there was no thought of lying, these were not people you lied to. The man went away again and Pete slept. He awoke to find two men grabbing his arms, a third slipped something heavy and foam lined over his head – some sort of helmet he thought with two tiny eye holes to look out of. Next, a one-piece suit was put on his struggling form, then boots on his feet and his hands jammed into large heavy gloves. Some sort of radiation suit perhaps, he thought. Were they going to make him work in a nuclear reactor? After that two guards took him to the surface in an elevator and then they let him go. He couldn't believe it, they just walked away. All he needed was a friendly face, somebody he could explain his situation to. If he could just get out of there then he'd blow the whole story open wide, he'd be life president of Libertad, after that, fuck it, he'd be life president of fucking Mexico! A friendly face! Pru obviously looking for him, her eyes looking this way and that, searching the crowds. Closing time was coming up and all the hot dogs were filing out, happy and glowing. Pete forced his way through the throng, reaching Pru he tried to embrace her and tell her of his ordeal. All she saw was the big-headed cartoon animal that looked like a dog but wasn't a dog waving its paddles at her and all she heard was a distant mumbling from deep inside its big silly cartoon head. She easily pushed it off and carried on frantically looking for Pete as the last sky rockets of the night exploded overhead, a million sparks drifting slowly and gently to earth.

LOCKED OUT

It was only when she got to her front door that Katherine realised she didn't have her keys with her. They were inside the house, snug in the pocket of her other overcoat, the fawn Nicole Farhi one. Not that much of a problem. Though it was a cold November night her car was parked there at the kerb, she could just sit in it until her husband came home from the university where he was a lecturer in philosophy. That would be in about three hours' time, at eleven o'clock. She blipped the door lock of her BMW 3 and climbed back behind the wheel. After few seconds she started the engine and turned the heater up, it was cosy in there, another button reclined the leather seat a little, this was nice, this was really nice, she should get on the mobile and make some calls or look over some case notes but, sod it, it felt good to just sit there. Her eyes drifted up the street, it was odd she thought, she'd never actually sat outside her own house before. All she ever did was cross the pavement to her car or walk to the corner to hail a taxi, sometimes she might walk the hundred yards to the Asian mini-mart to buy a paper or a packet of Hobnobs but that was about it. She had lived in this street for nearly ten years without ever looking at it for more than a few seconds. So what did she see now? A long row of elegant, four-storey, early-Victorian town houses and facing them a large private square with London plane trees reaching blackly into the night sky, higher than the houses they shaded. Beyond the square there was the outline of more trees, for though this was in the very centre of London, a brisk fifteen minutes' walk to the West End, bizarrely the street was on the irregular edge of several acres of grass and woodland. The street's garden square backed on to a children's playground complex established in the seventeenth century with playing fields, tall oak trees and bushes, behind that to the west was a council park, grass that should be on anti-depressants but some substantial yew and sycamore trees and plenty of dense wild scrub, hawthorn hedge and holly bushes. Also to the north of the street was a graveyard the Victorians had converted to a garden, a limestone angel watched over flower beds, winding paths and more trees. Living amongst all this verdure was the usual urban wildlife: squirrels, foxes, rabbits and schizophrenics who had forgotten to take their medication.

Katherine though had not chosen the house for its rus in urb charms but rather for its proximity to the Law Courts. She was a solicitor specialising in libel, her firm, of which she was the youngest partner at thirty-seven, was in nearby

Bedford Row, the barristers she needed to see were in the Inns of Court that started at Grays Inn, which was at the bottom of her street, and her cases were heard at the Law Courts on the Strand. The whole area was like a legal shopping mall especially the Inns which, with their crooked houses, paved courtyards and antique gas lights, reminded her of Bicester Factory Outlet Shopping Village. Only the housing had not succumbed to the power of the legal pound. The five flats in the two converted houses where Katherine lived were all owned by various brands of lawyer, but apart from that all the adjoining houses were owned either by housing associations or were still what they had been since the war, anthills of flats carved out of the neo-classical elegance of the houses, at least that's what she assumed from the museum of doorbells from through the ages that hung off the doorjambs of the four or five houses she could see from her car. Even in her own house though there was no neighbourliness. She had met the other lawyers but all she really knew of the tenants in the building was the sound of their feet on the stairs, or in the hall outside, generally scurrying in or out. In fact, she hadn't seen any of them for nine months, they could have all moved out and been replaced by heavy-footed ballerinas or perhaps overweight chimpanzees for all she knew. At least she had met the other tenants in the houses. As for the other neighbours she didn't know any of them at all, she'd never been one for mixing with the people next door, popping in and out borrowing jam. Her friends, such as they were, were scattered all over London, mostly in ones and twos, she was always reading about these great roiling extended families that people seemed to have these days, stepsons from second marriages living with three lesbian partners next door to the grandparents of the first marriage and grandad's seventeen-year-old male lover and his two children. It wasn't like that in Katherine's crowd, who were either single women dotted all over the far-flung edges of the tube map, wedged into crappy flat conversions behind plywood doors, or the odd chastely married couple either childless or with a couple of pale succubi stomping in and out moaning and groaning.

The only one in her household who had known the area intimately had been her cat Monty, an unneutered tom cat Katherine had had since a kitten. Every night he would wake from his place behind the television, squawk to be let out of the window and swagger off towards the square. The last sight Katherine ever had of him was his balls swinging into the shadows, for, one morning, he didn't return. She had expected it of course, owning a tom cat is like being married to a First World War fighter ace, the life expectancy is not good, though at the back of her mind she had thought that he was so wise and smart that he could escape the car wheels and wild dogs that did for the average cat. Apparently not. She thought about him every day and still grieved for him.

The street was silent, its northern end was blocked off by traffic barriers so no cars came through, the odd cyclist or pedestrian hurrying against the cold was all the movement there was. She had been sitting there for about fifteen minutes when a Japanese four-wheel-drive drew up at the pavement, the woman driver got out and went into a house two doors up from her own. This vehicle had interrupted many of Katherine's evenings. Because of its torn fabric roof the car's alarm was easily set off and when it did let go it didn't have just one tone but reproduced every alarm sound that there was, like a sort of Greek meze of car alarm sounds, hoots, honks, a medley of disco tunes from the 1970s. Funny for about five seconds, then not at all for the next twenty minutes till it calmed down. 'This car is alarmed,' said a sticker on its window. 'Fucking hysterical more like,' Katherine used to think. It was funny though that she'd never seen its owner until now and she was surprised to see she looked like a fifty-year-old civil servant.

Over the next two hours Katherine learned more about her neighbours than she had in the previous ten years. She saw the man who owned the big Mercedes van that was parked over the road at night but was always gone in the morning, the possessor of the bike chained to next door's railings, the blind man she had often seen shuffling up the pavement who she now learnt lived right next door to her, the owner of the red Vauxhall Astra with the orange disabled sticker that was parked outside her house day and night on the yellow lines while she hunted high and low for one of the rare residents' parking bays that the car-hating Camden Council provided. She often had to leave her BMW a short bus-ride away. The 'disabled' driver of the Astra, a slim

135

young man in clubbers' clothes, locked his vehicle, skipped across the sidewalk and just before he reached the steps of his housing association dwelling, executed a perfect forward somersault up the steps, which brought him to his front door. 'Disabled my arse,' thought Katherine. Her perception of where she lived began to shift. Before this evening she had been the centre of her own universe but now she had an uncomfortable sensation of all the other lives that were going on around her, sleeping when she slept, breathing in and out in a rhythm along with her own. Her cosy warm feeling had somehow dissolved, now she badly wanted her husband to come home. She looked at her watch, it was ten o'clock, she couldn't believe how quiet the street was. Then a flicker of light a couple of doors down in one of the rabbit-warren houses, two men and a young girl came out. There was something incongruous and somehow frightening about this trio. The men were both in their thirties, dark and swarthy, the girl small pale and blonde, she couldn't have been more than fifteen, her face was a frozen mask though as she turned the streetlight caught a tear trickling down her cheek and matching it a trickle of blood that emerged from beneath her short skirt and ran down her leg. The three climbed into an old Saab and drove away. Katherine found that although it wasn't hot in the car she was sweating and her heart was pounding, her breath was coming very fast, with difficulty she managed to get it under control. She opened her window and sucked in the cold night air. Her wish that her husband would come home was now intense but there was still another hour before he came to let her in to the sanctuary of their apartment.

The next thirty minutes passed calmly enough and Katherine began to settle down, she thought 'Just a bit spooked that's all'. All the work she had back at the office was probably preying on her mind. Or was it some kind of bad karma? After all her job was to ruin somebody's day, those long brown envelopes she sent out, a size and a shape that nobody else in the world used so you knew you were in trouble right there, dropping on to someone's doormat, causing the heart to stop for a beat, maybe there was a price to pay for that. Looking up the empty street she saw a movement from the private square, a black shape opened the gate that you had to have a special, hard-to-copy, complicated key to open. The shape was a man, a tall red-headed man wearing thick glasses, he had some kind of belt around his waist from which objects seemed to be dangling. The figure passed close to her car before the man turned into a house two doors down and silently entered. Since he had passed her Katherine's mind had been frozen revving, screaming away in neutral, then slipping into gear she thought, 'What were those forms, jiggling on his belt? The heads of . . . cats?'

A nameless dread was travelling in an express lift from somewhere near her stomach to her brain, a bell pinged, the doors of the lift slid open and terrible fear sauntered out. Katherine knew that she would never be the same again, her world had tipped sideways and even if she ever got it back it was dented. Where was her fucking husband? To let her in so she could crawl into bed and pull the duvet over her head, then maybe it would be better tomorrow. Except she knew it wouldn't be. Another twenty minutes to sit there. Of course she could go for a walk, go along the dark path that slid through the trees at the top of the square. They had a good laugh about that, her and the thing that had got out of the lift and into her head, they both knew she wasn't walking down that path anytime soon.

Her husband found her on the dot of eleven, sweat still rolling down her forehead and staining through her blouse making the shapes of imaginary islands on her jacket. He helped Katherine inside and asked her what was wrong. She told him what she had seen and he had explanations for all of it, he was a kind man and loved her more or less but she had entered another country, an hysterical Latin country, where everything was shouting and wild gestures and sensible explanations counted for nothing.

MY SHRINKING CIRCLE
OF ACQUAINTANCES

I can hear them coming so I don't have much time to get all this down on tape, the phones aren't working, they must have cut the line. Teach me not to get a mobile . . .

How did I get into this fix? Pride. Pride and hauteur I suppose. I have always been proud that I wasn't born a small man. I am, it is true, a bald man, but to be a small man and a bald man would, I have always felt, have been too much to bear. I am of course of above average height, six foot one. I read once in a women's magazine about this club, called something like the Big Dick Club, a group of blokes, perhaps in Denmark, I can't remember, had got together because they had such enormous wangs . . . to join you needed a joint of at least seven inches. I was thrilled when I read that. Mine exceeded that by at least two inches, when fully extended of course. Then it struck me, maybe seven inches wasn't big at all, maybe these blokes were just saying seven inches was exceptional to make themselves feel better, I mean how could you check a thing like that? Could become gay I suppose but producing the tape measure while having sex would appear a bit strange even in those easy come, easy go circles. You can tell if you're tall though, simple matter of observation, count the number of bald spots you can see, if a party looks likes a decimated rainforest you're in the club.

When I left university I started a little theatre above a pub, it seemed the easiest thing in the world to do then, with a grant from the dear old GLC and lovely London Arts in the tipsy days of the Right to Work marches and Rock Against Racism. What plays we put on above that pub, headline grabbers like Jenka Holme's *Biting the Cock That Fucks You* and Martin Plitts' *Puke!* The first ever London production of *The Blood Sausage* by Manuelta Xttarra, the Portugese Lorca.

I believe there is a moment in people's lives when they become who they are. Before that moment they are but a prototype, one of those concept cars you see at the motor shows, all bumps and wings and excrescences that hold within their shape the next mass-market auto. I must have had friends before I started my theatre. It was like that Abba song *The Day Before Love Came* because I can't really remember. I was plunged into a whizzy whirl of actors, writers, critics and all that I grew close to were tall. My girlfriend, actress Nyla Tooms, was a strapping five feet ten, my best mate, a little-known Irish actor by the name of Liam Neeson was ... well you've all read the stories about Ewen McGregor (no midget himself) having to stand on a box to act with him in the *Star Wars* movie.

The pub below my little theatre still charges for drinks in the old pre-decimal currency: pounds, shillings and pence. Though of course the actual price of the booze is very 1999 if not 2006. Bemused tourists can find themselves being asked to hand over 'ninety-four and twenty sixpence, mate' in return for a couple of whiskies by the Australian bar staff, 'twelve bob and a farthing' for a packet of crisps or 'two quid thirteen and nine' for a bottle of lager. There's a lot of drug dealing going on in that pub, I wonder whether that's also done in the old money. Do people slide up to the dealers in there and say, 'Give us ten and a tanner's worth of that crack will yer old pal?' or do they sidle up to the old shape BMW Seven series with the gold wire wheels and black-tinted windows parked outside the boozer and whisper, 'I say old fruit, if you'd be so kind, I'd like seven guineas' worth of scag, don't ya know, pip, pip.'

Anyway through the years after show after show we'd carouse in that pub me and my tall mates. I was as happy as a man can be. I guess that's why I also stayed in this flat. Who wouldn't, what with the view and all? Originally, while I was at uni I rented two grimy rooms off the Golbourne Road W11, North Kensington, dog rough and dirty. I don't know why some roads in London qualify for the 'the'. The Fulham Road, the Edgware Road but not the Southwark Bridge Road nor the Ealing Road. The Council bought the house to knock it down and transferred me here to this tower block, where

I've been ever since. I felt safe here, the previous flat had been invaded by mice just before I left which freaked me out – I hated the thought of these little things scuttling about inside the walls. The walls and floor in the tower block were solid concrete so there was no chance of mice getting in there. Sometimes I'd worry that they might come up the rubbish chute which dropped your garbage down to the bins on the ground floor, but in twenty years they never did. Clockwork Orange Towers, Dawes Road, London SW6. Twelfth-floor flat, living room, two bedrooms and a view over London to die for, which I am doing.

I shouldn't knock it, it's not one of those blocks on a huge estate, there's just the two, mine and A Bout de Souffle Point, looming over the slate-topped streets of Fulham. From my living room I can see all the way to where south-east London snivels into Kent or Surrey or somewhere. In the other direction, from my kitchen sink, I can look Central London right in the eyeball. When the Sultan of Brunei is occupying the whole top floor of the Park Lane Hilton as he is wont to do he can wave at me while I wash up the Rice Krispie bowl. When I wasn't working I loved to sit at the almost floor-to-ceiling window in the main room, watching the number 11 buses, nose-to-tail crawl up the Dawes Road. Then some time in the 1980s, because only poor people use the bus, they shrank them to vehicles hardly the size of mini vans. They renumbered them 211s, shrank the drivers' wages and terminated the route at Fulham Broadway. That's what happens when you fail, things mostly get smaller.

Round about the same time as the buses started shrinking, the Uraguayan holding company that owned the pub below started bitching about taking back my theatre and turning it into a comedy club. The ungrateful fucks! All the people over the years I've brought in to their stinking boozer to be parted from their tanners and threepenny bits. I was so worried, I stayed up all night, chewing on my watchstrap and watching distant lightning strike the early morning golfers of Surrey. Then round about seven a.m. I had a flash of my own. Wouldn't it be great if you could get a Hollywood star to come to a little fringe theatre and do a play? I got on the phone to Liam in eleven p.m. LA where by then he was living with Natasha (five feet ten inches) and I suggested he might like to get back to his roots and tread the carpet tiles again. 'Think of it,' I said, 'the rush of a live audience, the power of that huge Irish frame blasting the Nellie theatre critics with his raw power and his Hollywood glow.' He let me down gently enough, saying that movie stars could not dim their luminescence by allowing the public within an exclusion zone of thirty feet and if I was ever in the San Fernando Valley he'd found a place that did great Guinness. Of course, a few years later when Kevin and Nicole and Glenn had shown that it was safe to do plays in London he came over to the Almeida and appeared in some shite about Oscar Wilde written by Mr Nicole Farhi but it was too late by then.

Not to worry, not to worry. The Uraguyan holding company sold the pub chain to a Rwandan mining conglomerate and the threat to my theatre went away, but some of the buzz had rubbed off. There wasn't the same life in the plays any more and it was around about this time that my girlfriend suddenly started to seem like a big lumpy giant and an evening spent with my tall friends felt like a night in a wind farm. I started to slide away from them and they let me go without a whisper of regret. I stole away from them with as little fuss as a wildlife cameraman crawling away from a herd of grazing giraffes. Instead, as a lover, I took up with a female stage manager of below average height, 'Hey lets measure ourselves for a laugh,' (five feet two inches) and I began casting my plays with similarly smallish actors. Which for a while led to a surprise jump in profits, as we could get away with smaller sets and could thus increase the seating capacity.

Now I don't want you to get the idea that despite my wholesale rejection of a whole social circle my friendship was in any way a feeble thing. Not at all, not at all. Very much the reverse. My friendship is a strong spotlight. When I turn it on to someone I'm taken with they are dazzled. I phone you most days and you come to wait eagerly for those calls. I really, really want to know what you're going to name the kitten that I gave you. There's no chance in the world, if you get sick, of me not visiting you in hospital, I'll be the greatest god dad your kids ever had. If I become your friend your life will jump up a gear. Roses will be rosier, chips will be chippier because this special, good-looking, funny, talented man is deeply and profoundly interested in *you*. Just don't grow, that's all.

So that was how most of the 1990s passed. I suppose you could say I was merely following the business practice of the times, I was downsizing. Then in 1996 the hammer dropped, the Rwandan mining consortium having passed on their stewardship of Britain's theatrical heritage to a chain of Belgian pet superstores. Overnight my lovely theatre where once 'we crammed within the wooden "O" the very arrows that did afright the air at Agincourt' became Chucky's Chuckle Butty. And I was out of a life.

My beloved block of flats seemed to fall apart at the same time as I did, all of a sudden loads of the windows dropped out and we were hit with a crime wave. The block did not have the most reassuring of histories. Perhaps because in Britain we were only used to building little houses, when the post-war, sky flat craze came along the constructors adopted continental system build methods which may have been fine in the sunny climes of Marseilles but didn't cut the moutard in rainy old, rusty old London. Clockwork Orange Towers was, and please excuse the paucity of the metaphor, built like a house of cards, walls resting on floors which in turn supported walls. When in an identical block in the East End a gas cooker blew itself up it took one whole corner of the building with it . Now if you open any built-in cupboard in my place you will see huge sections of girders and giant bolts, literally holding the whole pack of cards in place. Similarly the windows should have been looking out over the Bay of Naples not the Fulham Cross so they threw themselves to the ground, rotted through. Not to worry though, not to

147

worry. This was a council flat, they replaced the old wooden windows with nice new metal ones. I remember once I came home drunk from the theatre with a bottle of cider in my pocket which fell out while I was being sick in the toilet, smashing the bowl. Lickety split the council came round and fitted a new lav, we were spoilt really. They weren't as helpful with security at first. You could walk in and out of the flats and local youths were simply catching the lift up a few floors and kicking doors in. I felt panicked, I didn't want to be violated, it was the mice all over again. I got the police crime prevention officer to come round. He sniffed around looking for drugs or illegal firearms and finding none gave my flat the once-over. He said the only weak spot was my front door and suggested I got somebody in to reinforce it. Who could do that for me? He consulted his list of approved freemasons and a couple of blokes came round the next day to bolt on a steel plate covering my door, this just left a small unprotected fanlight between the top of the door and the ceiling of the corridor but as one of the blokes said, 'You'd have to be tiny to get through that gap.' Indeed you would. Anyway about six months later the Council fitted automatic doors and an entryphone system so I felt doubly safe, which was good because I didn't go out much.

Even the medium-sized crowd that were my friends suddenly seemed to be too big for me. To be taking up too much space even with their dainty little shoes, to be sucking up too much air even with their snub little noses, to be making too much noise with their squeaky little voices.

I figured they would let me leave them as easily as the tall people did but that was not the case. At first they called round or phoned, worried about me, though I didn't know what it had to do with them, then when their enquiries were met with blankness they turned nasty. I couldn't believe it! A selection of hits from the guilt collection on my answerphone, 'Hi this is Marlene calling just to let you know that I've got a six-year-old crying his eyes out here wondering where his Unky Mike is on his birthday.' 'Mike, it's Len, the tests weren't good, I wish you were here with me mate, all the nurses are asking after you and I don't know what to tell them.' This from the girlfriend, 'It's me . . . Oh fuck what's the point . . . (extended sobbing) . . . no, I'm all right now . . . (extended sobbing) . . . no really I'm fine . . . (extended sobbing).' I had a loaf thrown at me in Waitrose and the brake cables on my bike were cut when it was parked outside the all-night Bagel Bake in Finsbury Park.

It was sitting in my picture window listening to the phone warble unattended and staring down at the night bus weaving its way up Dawes Road that I wrote a play, I wrote it in my head then I ran to my computer and by the time the sun came up over the secret Ministry of Defence building at Earl's Court I had it finished. It was called *Aitch Ee Ell Ell*.

Faruz Sharif had pretty much been the dwarf of choice in television and theatre circles in the last few years, I arranged to have lunch with him at The Ivy. I'd cast him years ago in a production of *Ubu Roi* though I didn't have much to do with him at the time. Now he was a big star . . . for a dwarf.

I got there early and had a drink at the bar, he arrived a few minutes later. It was funny to see Tall Jeremy who runs The Ivy bending in half to talk to him. After five minutes of small talk, Faruz disentangled himself, came over and clambered up a stool to sit at the bar and drink a vodka martini with me, his stubby fingers rummaging over and over in the peanut bowl. By the time our table was ready there were a couple of cushions on the banquette to bring him up to eating level, The Ivy's the sort of place where that kind of thing is discreetly done. On the surface I was all business and gossip, underneath my body was quaking with pride, here was me in this restaurant having lunch with a dwarf! Nobody else was having lunch with a dwarf, everybody else was having lunch with a huge fat twat like themselves.

Faruz, I guess, was a pretty modern sort of dwarf. Like most people of short stature he was a victim of achondroplasia mutations (chemical changes) within a single gene. The condition may be passed from one generation to the next or it may result from a new mutation in a gene from average-sized parents. Nine out of ten children born with achondroplasia have average-sized parents, and no other family member is affected. (I learned all this doing volunteer work for The Little People of Britain.) He tried not to mix with others of his kind. He had a BA in politics and economics from Sheffield University, he had married and separated from a full-sized woman and their one child (normal size). A couple with one achondroplastic spouse and one average-statured spouse has a one in two chance of having a child with achondroplasia and a 50 per cent chance of having an average-statured child. If both parents have achondroplasia, there is a one in four chance of their having a child who inherits two altered copies of the gene that leads to achondroplasia – one from each parent. These children are said to have homozygous achondroplasia, or 'double-dominant' achondroplasia. This condition is almost always lethal in the first year of life.

Yet Faruz wanted to be famous so bad, so bad, and that unfortunately meant showbusiness. Though he hadn't exactly done *Snow White and the Seven Dwarves* in panto he'd come pretty close a couple of times and so he often found himself with other little folk shrinking from their crude impish behaviour. And even when he had a big success he wan't safe, theatres would often cast one black or one Asian or one dwarf or one Downs Syndrome in a play but it was always somehow the full-sized white guy who became the star and went on to fame and glory. After all, you can read what Danny Day Lewis is up to most days in the papers but have you seen the brown boy from *My Beautiful Laundrette* in anything recently? I don't think you have.

Aitch Ee Ell Ell would be different. 'ELL' or Extended Limb Lengthening is a surgical procedure that can be used to extend a little person's arms or legs. What happens is that metal pins are inserted into bone, and then the pins are attached to a steel frame. The frame for the legs is circular, for the arms flattened. Then doctors cut the bone with a mallet and a chisel, they gradually pull the bone ends apart with a motor or hand-crank attached to the frame. New bone growth fills the empty space at the rate of about one millimetre a day. The most any Little Person has gained is ten inches. The procedure is unbelievably painful, and it often lasts several years. The most common complications are bending or twisting of the bone at the site where it is cut, and nerve damage caused by the metal devices that are inserted into the bones resulting in paralysis of the limb. If the length is increased too much, the muscle and skin will be stretched too tightly over the limb. This locks the limb out, either straight or bent, and leaves the person unable to control the limb. The only way to overcome this problem is to go back into surgery and shorten the bone. Any time a major bone is broken or cut, there is a risk of releasing fat emboli into the bloodstream, which can cause death.

The play is about a dwarf's dilemma on whether to undergo the procedure. I didn't need to tell Faruz what this play could do for him, he could see it right away. After all, this wasn't a play with a dwarf in it, this wasn't a play in which a dwarf played a fucking wizard or something like that, this was a play actually about a dwarf, about the real life of a dwarf, about an awful dilemma a dwarf would face, whether to undergo terrible pain in order to join the heighted or to learn self-acceptance. To stay an imp for ever.

He loved it. He loved all the serious stuff. Of course actors always do, but he loved the funny stuff as well, the comical yet moving scene, for example, where the dwarf tries to get money from an automatic teller machine that he cannot reach by trying to stand on the stoned junkie who is lying at the base of it.

So Faruz was on board and we needed six other actors: three small, three normal. Jimmy Herc, Paul and Annie Stewart were the little people. Jimmy was a smutty bastard, sticking his head up women's skirts and all that thing. Faruz hated him at first, Paul and Annie were married and had a little baby of their own, it would grow up to be little but at least it had survived, their previous three had died of homozygous achondroplasia, one lasting for fourteen months. I became the kid's godfather of course, you know how it goes by now.

We held the first read through of the play at Faruz's apartment. In nearly every room there was a footstool for him to stand on and get things. Dangling from the light switches were long plastic rods, and the lock on the back door measured inches lower than on most doors. Parked in the driveway was Faruz's 1998 Alfa Romeo and if you peeked through the window you could see extension pedals that elevated the surfaces more than a foot. Jimmy fucked about and Faruz shouted at him, Paul and Annie sat sweetly on the low sofa nursing their tiny baby. They thought my jittery, red-faced excitement was induced by the feeling in the room that this play that I had written and would direct really had a big chance of being a huge success. But my excitement was being with them.

We all went up to Edinburgh with the show, staying in a single apartment, getting drunk and buzzed late into the morning, hot properties. One day we had a game of five-a-side football on the Meadows, dwarves versus white folks, I wanted to play with the little people but for some reason they wouldn't let me and that made me angry and upset. I resolved to try and win for my side, I've been a pretty useful and rather dirty midfielder for the National Theatre in many games against the Royal Court, the cast of *Cats* and the like but I found you can't knock a dwarf over, they just slid in and out of our feet with the ball and were five one up by half time. Another time, late at night in the bar of the Gilded Balloon Paul and Jimmy showed me the little lock knives they carried: American Gerbers, tiny versions of their rubber-handled survivor knives, made to dangle off key rings but in the hands of Paul and Jimmy looking sharp and lethal, shockingly to scale, as if some kids' TV doll: Postman Pat or Tinky Winky had suddenly pulled a blade.

After Edinburgh we got the transfer into the West End, the Vaudeville Theatre on the Strand, the big time. One night the stage door keeper told me Liam was in. God it was good to see the bastard! 'I'm sorry,' he said. 'I guess I was a bit of an arse that time, about when you wanted me to do a play.' 'Oh fucking forget it.' I said, 'What's done is done, let's go and get a fucking drink.' We went to this actors' club that's on an old Arctic explorers' boat moored off Blackfriars Bridge and we drank till the tide came in.

A guy from Miramax pictures came backstage a few days later and said he'd like to have lunch with me, he had a script I might like to direct. We went to The Ivy and the same day he biked the script over. He thought Bobby De Niro would be great, I felt Tim Robbins would somehow bring more to the role.

Faruz collared me after a matinée one afternoon perhaps three weeks later, I was rushing off, I'd got some tickets to a basketball game and I wanted to be gone. 'No,' he said. 'What no?' I replied. 'Think,' he said, 'think how little our hearts are,' he said. 'Think how easily they can be broken.' I pretended not to know what he was babbling about but that didn't stop him.

'You can't walk away from a little person. If you befriend us you take us on, we are not for your pleasure, a friend is not for pleasure.'

'What you're saying is a dwarf is for life not just Christmas?'

'We can't allow it to be done,' he shouted as I scampered out of the stage door thinking, 'Creepy little fuck.' I'd been calling into the theatre less and less of late now that the show was up and running and everything. I thought maybe I should hang about a bit more, massage a few midget egos.

I got my assistant to send everyone a nice big basket of muffins by special delivery but when I arrived at my office in the Vaudeville that afternoon I found my private toilet was totally blocked with a hideous goo of what I hoped was entirely muffin.

Obviously I had to put in some personal time with them. So a few nights later we all had a drink at Teatro, cast and crew. I hadn't really wanted to do it but I thought genuinely

155

we had a great time, just like the old days. However, when I got home I found the backs of my trouser legs had loads of tiny slashes in them below the knee, my own blood had soaked into my trainers and I hadn't noticed. I thought, 'Well sod them then the ungrateful little shits!' After that they just made me sick, I couldn't help it, their stumpy little forms wriggling around, let's face it they're not normal are they? Their mutant anger is proof of that.

I hardly went into the theatre then at all. The third time that I did Annie Stewart pushed me down the backstage stairs. It didn't appear that way to anybody else, of course. I was coming down she was going up, somehow she got under my feet like a troublesome cat and I fell twenty steps breaking my leg and landing me here in bed, in my flat, hog-tied. I saw her eyes as I went down, cold, cold. Still I hoped that might be it for the revenge of the Munchkins. A few bones broken, no hard feelings and everything all squared away, let's get on with our lives, we can all be big about this. But, of course, they couldn't.

A few minutes ago I heard the metal door to the rubbish chute clang open, even though I'm sure there were no footsteps going to or from it, I think that's what woke me.

It'll be like one of those Agatha Christie mysteries, a locked room, a fortress apartment block and a dead playwright. Oh yes, they'll kill me, I know the fury now that's compressed into those little frames.

They're over the front door now.

THE BAD SAMARITAN

A Londoner is always within six feet of a rat. Well let me tell you, it's closer if Valentina is around. Ooh back in the knife drawer Miss Sharp! I won't take it back, it's true. What kind of a rat is she though? 'Love Rat' is the one the tabs use but she isn't one of those. 'Hate Rat' doesn't do it, 'Compassion Rat' fits maybe, or 'Emotion Rat'. Strange thing is, if you'd seen us together, even now you'd never guess I equated her with a snickety rodent. For such a long time she was my best friend. I thought she was great because I was ignorant of her true nature; now I think she's awful. Her wicked character seems so clear to me now that I'm amazed nobody else in our crowd sees it but they don't, they think she's brilliant. They call her 'sassy' because she says whatever comes into her head and they say she's 'sexy' because she thinks everybody fancies her and they say she's 'smart' because she's really stupid and shouts a lot about her idiotic opinions. See, I'm the only one who has seen the black shape scuttling along the skirting board, the whiskery snout disappearing down the pipe, the tail in the lavatory bowl.

I know I'm going on and I've always been a bit like this, running hot and cold on people. Through school I had a string of best friends, I was a serial bestfriender. One after another they came and went – Tubby Dowling, Peter Pemberton, Leo Scher. Then I'd have some falling out with them, they'd betray me in some way and I'd never talk to them again. See, I'm getting better. I hate Valentina like poison but I still see her all the time, that's more grown up isn't it? In the old days we used to phone each other every day though, now I think about it, I always called her more than she had called me, not by more than a factor of 25 per cent though which I think is more or less negligible, a tolerable margin of error between firm friends. Then. One day I liked her, the next day I hated her. It was that sudden. But it wasn't. What happens I think now is that it's like a dam breaking. The weight of this calm water with ducks on it and young offenders kayaking builds up and up till the wall cracks and it's transformed, it becomes this dangerous force, a raging torrent of hate or water. Now I can't understand why other people can't see what she's like. I'm going on about this aren't I? I'm obsessing, I do that but it makes me mad that everybody in our set can't see how evil she is, they all think she's the cat's pyjamas.

I suppose it's just the way you interpret events. For example, whenever there's a couple in our circle that splits up Valentina's always there, offering help, offering advice, shuttling between one and the other, cooking and cleaning, feeding cats, and just let some nelly she knows show the first symptom of Aids. Sometimes Valentina gets there before the Karposi's sarcoma. If I was HIV positive and I saw V's Polo pull up I'd start to worry. So they all say, 'Isn't it amazing? Valentina's so good, giving all that time, giving all that effort, giving all that succour, giving, giving, giving of herself.' Now I see, of course, it's no more amazing seeing V at the site of an emotional train wreck than it is seeing a fat man at a £5.50 All You Can Eat Thai Buffet, what she's doing is she's feeding. She's feeding on the emotion, like a big fucking basking shark. She's hoovering up the pain and the turmoil, it bigs her up, and if you were to go back in time to before the emotional train wreck happened the security cameras might see a dark-haired woman putting concrete blocks on the line. That'd be Valentina, for it's not enough for her to hang around and wait for emotional turmoil to happen, she makes it happen, she creates it. Like there was a married couple in our crowd and she got pregnant. They'd been all right till then but he was American and she was French so their national characteristics started to come out. She wanted to carry on drinking and smoking and riding roller-coasters, he wanted her to basically lie down for nine months, eating cabbage with her legs up in stirrups. Still they would have worked it out but V got in there. She would get reports from the hospital and contort them to confirm the husband's fears, I'd see her there in her office, when our shifts coincided, making up crap with her tongue sticking out. By the time the baby was born it was in a one parent family.

The last day that I saw her we were walking down a corridor in the hospital. A young couple sat in one of TV rooms where the lung cancer patients go to smoke. The woman had given birth about twelve hours before but the baby was dead, they held each other and stared off into a barely tolerable future. Valentina indicated that she was going to go inside, I stayed and watched through the glass as she slid into the room in a way that was supposed to be unobtrusive while drawing attention to her like she was a circus parade and sat across from them staring at their faces, neck outstretched like some demented turtle. Finally, the man returned from whatever anteroom of hell he'd been in. 'Who the fuck are you?' he asked. 'Hello,' replied Valentina in a voice slick with sympathy. 'I'm Valentina the hospital psychologist. I'm here to offer you counselling.'

THE GOOD SAMARITAN

Dominic was tired and cold and all the biscuits he'd eaten had made him feel a bit sick and funny inside. It was now about four-thirty, already dark on this winter's afternoon behind King's Cross Station as he trudged back home to the tiny bedsit he inhabited south of the Euston Road. Dominic, tall pale and red-headed had spent the day working as a volunteer at the Camley Street Nature Park. Though maimed by depression and living on a disability pension he made himself go to the park every Wednesday, he wanted to do all he could to pay a little back to the world, the beautiful world.

Camley Street was as beautiful as the world got behind King's Cross Station. A former coal yard about an acre in size there had been plans to turn it into a coach park in the 1970s until the old GLC had stepped in and given two million pounds to the London Wildlife Trust who'd ploughed up the toxic land, put in a large lake fed from the canal that bounded it on one side, planted native trees and laid down a water meadow writhing in summer with wild flowers. Over twenty years later there was a mature English forest making a stand for prehistory amongst the waste dumps, gravel yards, grade-one listed gasometers and golf driving ranges that filled the wild land north of the rail tracks. Today they'd been pollarding cracked willow. Every five years or so these trees were cut back to their stumps, their thick branches chopped for fence posts, the smaller ones kept for latticing into the living fences that lined the paths, and the rest, 'the brash', chucked on a pile in the southernmost corner where one day the Eurostar Terminal was supposed to take a bite out of the park. The fence posts would be sprouting green shoots themselves by the next summer.

The volunteers got three pounds for expenses and all the Café Direct coffee and biscuits they wanted. Dominic always gave his three pounds back to the park even though the Volunteers' Charter said you weren't supposed to. Sometimes there were six of them sometimes only two. Today there'd been a nervy Dutch girl from a homeless hostel in Camden Town, obviously like Dom on some sort of medication, a young guy who'd just completed an Ecology degree and was keeping his hand in before he started work as a ranger at a science park outside Swindon and a hippy kid who Dominic guessed wouldn't be back again. Next week they'd go through the undergrowth picking up the syringes and empty wallets the junkies threw over the fence and the

Red Bull cans the clubbers chucked over coming back from Bagleys and The Cross on the other side of the canal.

He scuttled across the Euston Road, through Argyll Square where the dolies and the refugees stayed in the small hotels, the Celtic Hotel and the Athlone. Sorry, No Vacancies. Then he took the path that wound across the gardens, in between the council flats where all the Bangladeshis lived and after that another path that wandered between the tall London plane trees in Regent Square. Dominic was just about to cross over Guildford Street when he saw a businessman hurrying along, glance at something on the other pavement, hesitate for a second then walk on. Dom looked in the same direction. In the grey light a figure was lying on the pavement, going closer he saw that it was an old man, he wore a mac and underneath that a thick jumper plus a Nike cap twisted by his fall so that it was now almost homeboy backwards. By his side were a couple of bags of shopping from the Safeway store in the Brunswick Centre and a shooting stick. Dom touched the man lightly on the shoulder saying, 'Are you all right mate?' Instantly his eyes opened and he said in a wide-awake voice as if asking the time, 'Did I black out again?' Then confusion settled on him again. Dominic managed to get the man upright, he had cut his head when he had fallen. A very nice student came along and the old man said maybe they could get him a taxi but the student went to the ambulance station in Herbrand Street and ten minutes later a paramedic came along on a big Honda, mumbling into his helmet. Dominic sat with the old man who told him he had cancer, a hernia and a heart condition until the ambulance came for him and took him away. He stood and watched as the vehicle slid away, all the slender hope and energy that his day's work at the park had conferred ran out of him to lie in a pool on the pavement next to the blood from the old man's head wound. He forced himself to move even though he could have easily stood there for the rest of his life. Like a rusty robot he ground his way to the Safeway store to buy some pilchards which he hoped he'd summon up the lust for life from somewhere to eat for his tea.

Outside the supermarket a girl from the crusty brew crew who hung around drinking on the steps of the Brunswick Centre was begging. The Scottish alky accent she'd learnt couldn't quite cover up the lilt of the stockbroker belt as she, spotting a mark, said aggressively to Dominic, 'Gor anny spear change mate?'

He didn't, he only had enough for his pilchards, 'Sorry no,' he said.

She looked at his hunched beaten form.

'You selfish cunt,' she said.

LOSE WEIGHT, ASK ME HOW

'. . . in and tonic would be fablious yes. Very kind of you I must say to buy a fellow a drink . . . erm? Oswaldo . . . you're Spanish I'm guessing? Here for the antique market tomorrow morning? . . . No I just guessed, we get a lot of Spanish, Italians, Germans coming over to buy antiques, take 'em back to their own countries, tidy little profit and no questions asked, eh? No need to worry round here mate, centuries old tradition of larceny. Murder, smuggling, prostitution, *Oliver Twist* wasn't set in these parts for nothing. Changed a bit now of course. All the old warehouses and tanneries down Bermondsey Street are antique places, well some are being made into loft style apartments. Do they have them in Madrid? . . . No, thought not, bit of a bloody silly idea really. My name's Graham, pleased to meet you Oswaldo. Do you know the history of the market? People say if you sell something at the market before the sun comes up and it turns out it's stolen then you can't be done for receiving, a sort of Middle Ages thing, that's why it starts at 4 a.m. Load of bollocks, cojones you know. The market came here to Bermondsey Square in the 1920s, used to be round the Great Caledonian Meat Market, up at Holloway, closed down during the First World War so they came here. Staying at the Holiday Inn in Rotherhithe? Yeah a few of the dealers and other single businessmen stay there, some pitch up here to this pub. Go for an early evening stroll up the river, gets dark, they get lost, nothing around but railway arches and gloomy warehouses. Panic, it being somewhat bleak around these parts, specially on a foggy night such as this, see the pub all lit up and cozy, coziness being a relative term if you know what I mean, Oswaldo, and pop in. Takes a bit of nerve though or a failure to grasp the subtle signifiers that say 'rough boozer, stay well clear', I tell you, Oswaldo, if you were at home you would run a mile from the Madrid branch of Simon the Tanner. Actually, it's all right now but it used to be a bloody rough old dive, much better now, new landlord see, the old one was a right fucking bastard but he disappeared. What's the Spanish for cunt . . . is it really? I must remember that for if I ever meet Antonio Banderas eh?

Interesting story though, the last landlord . . . no let me pay for this one . . . Gerry same again . . . Cheers, *salud*, I used to be able to say cheers in about twenty languages – '*Saha*', that's it in Arabic, wouldn't think Muslims would say cheers but there you are, '*Kipis*', that's Finnish, now those cunts do drink. Part of my job in a way . . . no, hah ha I'm not a professional drinker but the next best thing . . . motoring correspondent . . . *Auto Mail*, know it? We have a deal with your own '*Noticias Des Coches*', I tell you compadre it is the life and no mistake. That's why I bought the flat in the block next door, did you see it . . . Tanners Yard, converted tannery . . . lovely big flats, I know I went on about lofts but these are just lovely big flats, lovely metal Victorian windows and ironwork, stripped wooden floors. Thing that appealed to me though was the secure parking . . . the whole basement is one big car park . . . automatic gates, CCTV surveillance. See, in my job I've got a different flash motor every week and a lot of them you can't leave on the street. Imagine, stick a Bentley Azure Continental or a Subaru Impreza Turbo outside this boozer, David Copperfield couldn't make it vanish faster. So I was dead keen on the place and a pub next door, couldn't be better, would have been better without Richard . . . the old landlord. To look at me now you wouldn't think that once I was a fat man would you? . . . No indeed that's very kind of you. I was though, very fat indeed. It's the job you see, they fly us out to all these fablious places, the car makers, and they wine and dine us, wine, wine, wine and dine, dine us. Putting on weight though, you put it on then you can't take it off. It's like those people in the old days who stole a loaf and were transported to Australia for life, for this tiny crime. You eat a delicious tagine of baby lamb and dried fruits at the launch of the Talbot Solara in Agadir, remember them? Bloody good on paper . . . shit on the road! Actually shit on paper as well. Anyway, you eat this meal and you put on the fat and it won't bloody go away, honestly I could point to a roll of fat and say, 'Morris Marina roll out . . . roast pheasant and a Montrachet '47 or Toyota Supra launch, California '89, blue fin tuna in a salsa verde and a bathful of Napa Valley Chardonnay.' I'll tell you a secret of my trade, the worse the car, the better the launch. If you've got a brilliant car then you can make journos come to you, they never roll out Mercedes in Tuscany, they fly you to Stuttgart for an afternoon and you can like it or lump it. If you've got a dog of a car then different rules apply. Then, you get the hacks locked up on some paradise island for a week, they're bound to write about your motor because they've wasted a week of magazine time in the Caribbean, see? Oh there's been some larks on those trips . . . I've personally written off a Daewoo Leganza and a Mitsubishi Shogun and old Billy Ketts of the *Express* was doing a photo shoot at sunset on the beach at Cannes with the Mark Two Granada, when the fucking tide comes in. Well the old Mark Two granny was a good enough motor in its way but it didn't fucking float, I can tell you that for nada.

All the time the weight is going on and on. I jogged, I lifted weights, I did aerobics. Nothing made any difference. Plus I'm a sociable chap, have a deep craving for the company of other fellows in a shallow, meaningless and uncommitted sort of way. Pub's perfect for that, as long as you don't think that pub friends are real friends. Downside is, pub friends can be rather nasty in a jocular way if you've got any sort of imperfection. They fasten on to it. Holocaust mentality masquerading as matey joshing. So they were always going on about the fatness, here in Simon the Tanner, fatness being considered fair game even though it's recognised as a genuine medical condition by the American Medical Association. I mean if there was somebody in this pub who was an amputee they wouldn't call them 'stumpy'. Well, they probably would in here but you take my general point? The bleeding landlord, the governor was the worst . . . Richard always going on about who ate the pies . . . empanadas you call them Oswaldo. 'You're looking porkier Graham you fat bastard, you fat bastard, you fat bastard.' Obesity though, it's the curse of our age isn't it? I mean your Edwardians could eat those huge breakfasts without putting on an ounce, talk about your full English, full continent of Europe more like! It's got to be said cars are at fault for weight gain, cars and central heating to my mind because your Edwardians, they walked everywhere and they were always cold in them big houses. It's the holy grail isn't it? A way to hang on to all our comforts and stay slim? What would people do for that, eh Oswaldo?

All that fat stuff got me down, in the end I started going to other boozers, one particular one down by your hotel. Spice Island it's called, big barn of a place, lovely girls behind the bar. I have to admit, Oswaldo, that I often drove down there, very bad when you're drinking, no excuse for it really apart from the bastard landlord here had forced me into it. So, anyway, one night I'd had a skinful at Spice Island

and I was driving back along Bermondsey Wall, I had the new Volvo C70 coupé, bit of a disappointment to my mind, doesn't give you what they call 'the lob on', if you catch my drift. I'm sticking to the quiet streets along the river so the coppers don't catch me because obviously a ban would be the end of my so-called career. When suddenly this arsehole on a penny farthing bicycle swerves into my path! Honestly Oswaldo, I didn't have any time at all to react, I just smashed straight into him. He crashes head first on to the cobbles. I jam on the anchors go back to take a look. Turns out it's Richard on his way back from one of his fucking moronic Masonic drinking clubs. Mister Pickwick's Bicycle Society. Well that straw boater did not offer much crash protection I can tell you, he was dead Oswaldo, dead as a doorknob.

Want to go Oswaldo? Why's the door locked? It's what's called 'a lock in', see we still have these stupid drinking laws in this country. Legally, this pub should have stopped serving an hour ago, so everybody has to be locked in, in case the coppers come around — it'll seem all quiet from the outside. Nothing to worry about, go on have another drink . . . there you go . . . now where was I? Oh yeah, so he's lying there and there's no way I can get caught with him, so as I said in my review 'for a sporty 2.5 turbo-charged coupé the C70 certainly has a capacious boot, capable of swallowing several bags of golf clubs or one dead fucking cunt of a publican,' I didn't write that last bit of course. I chucks the penny farthing into the Thames, then what I do is I sticks him in the boot and I drives him back here, next door, to the underground car park of my block. Now at that time I was the only one living in the entire block, I'd moved in before the building work was completed. The developers had got into some sort of dispute with the builders and they walked off the job so work hadn't progressed for about three months. The car park was completely empty . . . not much changed from when it was the cellar of the tannery. I still had to hide him though. What I did was I dragged him out of the boot and I had a shufty around. In one corner I find a load of tools left behind by the tanners: rusty knives and saws and implements for doing God knows what to a carcass. So I gets one of the saws, then I chops him up into bits, head, legs, arms, torso, that sort of thing till he was sort of a kit of Richard. Then I stuffed his bits up one of the chimneys that they had down there. By then it was 3 a.m. I was pissed, I was in shock and I was knackered, I just needed to sleep on it then I'd figure out what to do with him, so I went to bed.

Had one of the best night's sleep I've ever had, to tell you the truth, straight nine hours. Got a shock when I woke up though, the fucking builders were back! I staggered down to the basement and I nearly shit! They'd lit a fire under Richard! They were burning scraps of the oak floorboards. Furthermore I couldn't get to him at night because they'd put this idiot Geordie security man in there. Always prowling about with his mangy Alsatian. I tell you every day I was expecting the police to pull me in. They kept burning wood in that fireplace as well, until I had a bit of luck, after a couple of weeks the builders fell out with the developers again and they quit. So I was able to go and get him that night. If you're wondering by the way if he'd been missed, the answer is not that much. Publicans are always going missing, it's that kind of game, attracts that kind of person, itinerant you see. Usually they scarper with the week's takings but seeing as he hadn't nobody was mounting too much of a search. As far as anyone was concerned he'd just vanished into fat air.

When I got him down from the chimney that night, guess what? He'd been smoked! Smoked like a kipper! Smoked just like your own Jamon de Serrano, I remember we had some lovely slices of that when they launched the Fiat Uno. Well I have to say I did a strange thing then, I carved myself a slice of him and I popped it in my mouth. Tasty, very tasty but filling too. A couple of slices and I felt full up, there always was only so much of Richard that I could take. Thing was, I felt energetic too, I hauled him upstairs to my flat bit by bit and I hung him in a cupboard.

Over the next few weeks I found that if I had a couple of slices of smoked Richard in the morning then I didn't want to eat anything for the rest of the day. I was happy to turn down all the snacks and titbits that had blobbed me out before. Plus I was absolutely brimming with vigour, I hadn't felt so well for years. I looked great too, sleek and confident, a fat man who's lost his fat is a happy man. The pounds fell off me until I was down to my perfect weight.

Gerry here replaced Richard at the pub, a much more genial fellow and life was good. Two things though. Pretty soon folk started asking me what my secret was and I started to run out of Richard. Now it would obviously be a risky business for me to try and replace him on my own, so after a while a solution occurred to me. What I did was I quietly asked around until I'd recruited a network of wealthy clients who wanted to remain sleek and svelte while partaking of the good things in life. Then I collected a crew of helpers from around these parts, only a variation on what they'd been doing for centuries if you think about it. Finally as for erm . . . what you might call the raw material . . . well foreigners that nobody is going to miss, dodgy characters without attachments are a good start . . . did you like that last drink, Oswaldo? Haven't been able to move your legs for the last couple of minutes have you? Arms are heavy too. That's right, well it should reach your brain at any mo . . .'

THIS STUPID SMILE

'. . . man in punt, man on bus, bloke in chiller cabinet at supermarket, you Tom of course and did we do it Miles? If you say so . . .' Ellie Aushwitz was trying to recall for the group seated around the table everybody she had ever had sex with. The woman had been talking without interruption for ten minutes and didn't look like stopping any time soon. '. . . butcher's assistant, RAC man who came to fix my . . .' Their conversations seemed to take this sort of smutty, slightly nostalgic course much more often these days. Now the group was in their early forties. When they'd been in their twenties and having sex all the time they'd never talked about it at all.

This took place at a restaurant in Clerkenwell. It was a Saturday night and maybe because of the odd day, their Clerkenwell was more of a Monday to Friday sort of place and the streets outside were dead, the service was poor and the food was poor but they had a good time, they took their good time with them wherever they went.

Harry Sharp was a new recruit to the group, he thought they were great, though of course he didn't let this show, he knew better than that, he'd been round the block enough to sense that enthusiasm was next to fascism in this gang's philosophy. Harry was a musician or rather he thought of himself these days as somebody who worked with music. After leaving university he had spent fifteen years playing guitar with most of the top rock acts, he'd got to fly in the same private 747 as Madonna and the Stones and Bowie. He'd slipped out of that to do incidental movies for TV and films. Only in this new game for a couple of years, his reputation was growing and most days he spent at the top of his house in Hackney with his computer and a stack of videos of time-coded dramas concerning the ups and downs of ambulance men and firefighters and cops.

He had his own circle of friends, like himself from the warrior caste of the rock business: keyboard players on a wage, roadies, sound engineers, and they had probably done a lot more in their lives than these new people he was with, they had taken more drugs, fucked more people, been to more strange places, had more adventures than this group. Thing was though, with his friends they couldn't make anything out of their lives. Events of the most astonishing complexity had happened to his mates (especially the roadies), but all they could do is tell you about it, recount a series of stuff that had happened, they could draw no moral, they could perceive no matrix.

Now this gang around the table, they could weave a tale out of a trip to the newsagents. They were: Ellie Aushwitz, she presented things, she presented TV programmes on fashion or motoring or anything, she presented corporate evenings, sometimes she presented awards to people. She had been at university with Agnes Trudeau who now ran and part owned the production company Bussman's Holiday, which made some of the programmes that Ellie presented, Agnes's ex-husband and co-owner of the company was Miles Bussman who was also there. Miles had lived with Ellie for a couple of years during which time she had presented him with a baby, which now lived with Ellie and Tom Archekowski, the fourth guest, an architect currently working on a house for Miles. There were also two gay guys at dinner, Mike and Marc. Mike worked for Agnes as a producer and Marc worked in a shop but was nevertheless 'good value'. The reason Harry had been invited along was that he was doing the music for a show Ellie was presenting and they had got along very well, after a quarter-hearted attempt on her part to get him to sleep with her, she had decided he might make a friend and being a friend of hers involved being friends with these six around the table and about twenty others as yet undined with.

That was another problem with his friends, they didn't particularly get on with each other so they all had to be seen singly and each of them wasn't quite interesting enough to fill up an entire evening. So although he was out every night at bars and restaurants and gigs he felt deeply unsatisfied and by the time he'd finished seeing his small circle of mates it was time to start all over again at the beginning. Ellie's gang in contrast went everywhere together, and linked by a thousand shared nights their conversation swooped and dove around Harry's head.

After the meal they stood outside the restaurant and said their goodbyes under the curly neon sign on the empty pavement before getting into their cars. On the other side of the Clerkenwell Road, about a hundred metres away, a huge queue snaked its way into the entrance of an old warehouse. This was a club called Turnmills. A famous DJ none of them had heard of was on tonight. While Ellie's friends were going home to bed for those in the queue the evening hadn't started yet.

The time was around eleven thirty, Agnes said 'so long' first and after twelve kisses detached herself from the group and walked towards the silent square where her black Jaguar XK 8 coupé was parked. When she got to the car she blipped the lock and was just about to climb in when a dented dark brown Toyota Corolla pulled to the kerb ahead of her, she had a slippery memory of this same car slicing past a few minutes before while they had been chatting outside Jean Christophe's place. Three compact swarthy men got out of the car with a choreographed sense of purpose, grabbed her. One around the head another taking the waist, the third going for the legs. She left the ground before she really took in what was happening but then she began to struggle. If you have ever tried to take a cat to the vets and it has wanted to escape from your grip then you may know what it was like to try and hold on to Agnes Trudeau. Every gym-toned sinew swelled like iron and she began to writhe, sinuous and desperate. The hand slammed over her mouth smells of lemons, she sinks her teeth into it, for a second it withdraws and she screams. The group standing outside the restaurant hears her scream, they look to where she struggles with the three swarthy men and they do nothing, absolutely nothing, they can't take it in.

Violence, sudden random violence, was so unknown to them that any other explanation as to what was happening up the road popped into their minds before the true one. Had Agnes met some mates who she was so pleased to see that she had started uncontrollably screaming and dancing about? Maybe that wasn't Agnes up the road at all but some woman wearing Agnes's clothes who looked just like Agnes and who didn't for some reason want to get into her friends' horrible brown car.

If the gang of six had been BT engineers or roadmenders or bakers then they would have known instantly what was going on, instead they just stood there while stranger and stranger scenarios whirled round their heads and their friend came closer to terrible danger. OK, as with any group of six people from that class, income bracket and general occupation, two were taking some type of Prozac drug, so perhaps too much couldn't be expected of them. Still though.

Only Harry reacted, he sprinted up the street and hurled himself towards the struggling threesome. In Celine Dion's band the drummer had been a devotee of the Chinese boxing style known as Wing Chun, a devastating short form of Kung Fu that specialises in a flurry of blows, mostly to the head, control of the opponent's arms, and constant unrelenting attack. It is very intimidating. Harry and the drummer had spent hour after hour practising the Su Lim Tao, the 'small thought form' in between sound checks and Harry had kept up the classes once or twice a week ever since.

Reaching the squat man who had a grip of Agnes's legs and was trying to stuff them into the back seat of the Toyota, Harry launched himself into what is known as 'front heel kick', an economical low kick designed to break the opponent's knee. He missed by at least six centimetres, unbalanced and offcentre, his momentum carried him pitching forward, he head butted the man in the backside, a move for which there was no name in Chinese or English, though effective enough in that it caused the man to drop Agnes. The man turned and swung a punch, Harry attempted the block known as 'fuk sau', he knew it hadn't worked when his ear started burning and blood sprang from his head.

Now that Agnes could get her feet on the ground her struggles became even more violent, the two men didn't know whether to stick with her or to try and take on Harry. The one that he was already dealing with reached behind him and pulled out a knife with a wooden handle and a curved, needle-sharp blade, perhaps legitimately connected with the carpet laying trade. He swung it at Harry in a curving arc, and, being too slow to get his head out of the way the knife tore through his cheek, across his mouth and slit his other cheek. The pain was intense, the only good thing, if you can call it that, was that Harry's attacker was now positioned with his arm straight across his body ready to slash backhand in a way that was highly vulnerable for the move known as 'lap sau'. For the only time in his life it came together. Harry took the man's wrist in his right hand, pointing his fingers back to the shoulder, thumbs in back of his hand while pressing the elbow joint with his left palm. Forcing the trapped elbow upwards tore the man's arm out of its socket and he bellowed with pain as Harry forced him to the floor delivering an elbow strike to the temple as he went down. When he was on the ground Harry still held him there straight armed and stamped on his head till he went quiet.

As the swarthy man sobbed into silence man one and man two decided without words being spoken to give up on their abduction of Agnes and to kill her rescuer instead, they would have done it as well if a couple of the doormen from Turnmills hadn't finally seen what was going on in the distance and come bundling up in their black bomber jackets like a pair of malevolent Michelin men, skittling Tom and Ellie out of the way as they came. This was what they did, these men, this was their job. An event for Harry and Agnes and the three swarthy men that was life contorting, for the doormen would hardly be remembered in a couple of days. Just another day at the deli counter. That was what it was like, for they dealt with the two swarthy men as if they were a pair of bored assistants at Safeway doling out tubs of houmous and weighing packets of Scotch eggs . . . switch, slick, click and the two assaulters were lying on the floor quietly crying for their mothers. 'Nice lap sau,' one of the bouncers said to Harry then indicating his splayed open cheek. 'You should get that seen to mate.'

The police told Miles that the three men in the Toyota had already abducted and murdered two women. Agnes would have been next if Harry had not stopped them. Miles told this to Agnes and Agnes told this to Harry when she went to visit him in the hospital. He had been taken to Bart's A & E department but as soon as he was stitched up Agnes had him shipped by private ambulance to the same exclusive joint where she had had her nose done and her craving for cocaine dealt with.

To Harry the room he was in at the Nightingale was exactly the same as all the rooms he had stayed in while he'd been touring with XTC or Elvis Costello, the TV on a bracket screwed high up on the wall, the pointlessly complicated curtains that didn't close, the room service menu with prices 50 per cent higher than they would be in the streets outside and, most of all, the fact that somebody else was paying.

He sat in bed, his wound now stitched up and await-ing plastic surgery gave the appearance of a huge grin stretching across his face. People who came to visit him thought subconsciously, because of that smile, that they were being terribly witty and amusing the whole time. Many remembered their visits to Harry in the hospital as one of the high spots of their month. Agnes felt she had so much to say to him, 'I simply cannot start to even begin to thank you enough,' she said, a pause . . . 'You saved my life.' And he said, 'No really it was nothing.' And smiled. Miles, Tom, Ellie, Mike, Marc, a woman call Crystal and a small child who seemed to be called Boundary all murmured that he was a hero.

Maybe he was, inside he felt that it was a lot more than nothing, it was a lot but he couldn't say so, he sensed again that that would be bad manners. Plus, what would be the point? There was really nothing Agnes could buy him in gratitude that he didn't have already, his career was going fine, he didn't need her help with that. She could buy him a car or something but that would be both too much and not nearly enough. The more he brooded on it he realised he had done this incredible, unbelievable thing for another person. Her life would really have ended soon after she had been hauled into that brown Toyota of death. He had handed her entire existence back to her by fighting with those men and getting his face slashed open and there was nothing she could do to repay him. He didn't even like her that much any more. Agnes and her posse of friends had been to see him quite a few times, had been very diligent in their visiting in fact, in their visiting and in their gifting. On the second day his room had been choked with flowers and cards and baskets of muffins from them, delivered by companies that specialised in these things. Yet in this situation, with him plastered with his stupid smile, whatever there had been that night had evaporated, they were now just some annoying posh people, some posh annoying people. One of whom he had given the precious gift of life to and in return she had given him a basket of muffins.

Agnes was at her desk a couple of weeks later when the phone rang. 'Bloke called Harry Sharp wants to talk to you,' her PA said. 'Harry who?' she was about to say, then she remembered. 'Put him through, always put him through,' she said instead. Then, 'Harry how are you? You seemed a little down the other week when I came to the hospital.'

'I'm a bit better now,' he replied.

'What did the consultant say about the scar?'

'He said there's always going to be a faint mark but in time after three or four reconstructions, as he called them, it shouldn't show too much.'

'That's good. You know I'd be happy to pay for it all,' she said.

'No point,' Harry replied. 'The consultant himself said that at this level of surgery the National Health is better than any private hospital. Look, I called because I wanted to talk to you about something else.'

'Sure,' she said, her PA was waving at her, mouthing that she had a meeting with Harry Enfield's agent in fifteen minutes. Well he could just wait, this was the man who saved her life.

'Do you know the Landmark Hotel?' He asked her.

'On the Marylebone Road, near Baker Street?'

'That's the place.' He said sounding pleased. 'It was a big old railway hotel that was completely done up a few years ago, it's very swish now. They've got this huge atrium at the centre of it that they call the Winter Garden, live fifty-foot palm trees and everything. Now they do this afternoon tea there, it's seventeen pounds, which I think is way too pricey but there you are. Anyway I thought we could have tea there, maybe next week or the week after, soonish anyway and sometime during the tea I could get my cock out and you could get down on your knees and suck it till I came.'

She found herself thinking, 'Next week could be difficult because it's the MIP TV festival at Cannes but the week aft . . . wha! Suck your . . . get down and have tea and get out your palm tree . . . seventeen pounds in the old railway cock?' She said. 'What?'

He said, 'Sometime during the afternoon tea I could get my cock out and you could get down on your knees and suck it till I came.'

She said, 'Why?'

He said, 'Because I saved your life and this is how you can repay me.'

She thought for a bit. 'Is it that you want to fuck me? We could take a room at the Landmark Hotel I guess and we could do it there. I'd be happy to, if that's what you want.'

'No that's not it at all,' he replied, sounding peeved. 'You're a very good-looking woman Agnes and all that but I don't fancy you. I just want you to give me a blow job in public. Your friend Ellie said she'd done that in Westminster Abbey the night I saved your life and you laughed like a drain. Look, I'm sitting here with this stupid smile carved in my face and it's hard to go out these days, I get frightened and nothing makes much sense to me at the moment and I want you to do this for me. I know you won't like it much, we'll get thrown out by the security. Probably before I come so you won't have to worry about your clothes getting messed up . . .'

'People know me though, word will get around.'

'Sure,' he said. 'In fact I thought I might get a photographer down from one of the tabloids, take a photo so it would get in all the papers. It'll be horribly embarrassing. Won't kill you though, will it? Won't kill you like those men were going to do. Groupie did it to me once in a hotel in Phoenix, it was a laugh, no big thing. You'll still be alive afterwards and the bottom line is you wouldn't have been alive if I hadn't fought with those blokes. You'd be dead.'

After a pause. 'Can I think about this?' she asked.

'Of course, take your time, give us a bell when you've made up your mind,' and he rang off.

His phone rang at 2 a.m. the next night.

'Ellie Aushwitz says what you're doing is the same as what those blokes were going to do to me before they killed me.'

'Well I don't think that's true at all, do you?' he replied. 'I can see that it might not be nice for you, horrible even, but it's not the same as those blokes. Not the same at all. I saved your life and it cost me a lot.'

'I'll ring you back.'

'Night night.'

The next night the gang all had dinner at a place near Smithfield Meat Market where your Pacific Rim fusion food comes wrapped in last week's Tokyo newspapers.

'See Konishki won the big Sumo basho in Kyoto,' said Miles.

'Stop fucking showing off Miles,' said Ellie. 'It's obvious that he hates and fears all women and he wants to humiliate us all by making a powerful woman like Agnes dance naked around the lobby of the Holiday Inn playing with herself.'

There was no need to ask who 'he' was.

'No, it's a blow job at the Landmark Hotel,' said Tom.

'Same thing,' said Ellie riding over him.

'He did save my life,' murmered Agnes tentatively.

This made Marc really mad. 'That was ages ago!' he more or less screamed. 'The guy's got to stop living in the past. Get a life, move on for fuck's sake.'

All night they argued it back and forth but they came to no conclusion apart from that haddock doesn't really go with Thai glass noodles.

The next week Agnes had to go to the MIP festival in Cannes but as soon as she got back she phoned Harry.

'Hi, how's it going?' she asked.

'Not great,' he replied 'I'm on anti-depressants that the doctor's given me.'

'Oh I'm sorry,' she said.

'I got a phone call from your friend Marc in the middle of the night.'

'Oh Christ! I'm sorry.'

'He said he knew where I lived. I said I knew where he went to fuck schoolboys. He screamed and I think he dropped his mobile phone in the river.'

She laughed. 'I'm still thinking about it you know.'

'Good.'

'It'd be horrible.'

'That would be the point.'

'Bye then.'

'Night, night.'

She didn't see or speak to him for nearly a year and when she did he was coming out of the Landmark Hotel as she was going in.

'Oh . . . er . . . um this is embarrassing,' she said.

'Don't worry they won't be serving tea for another four hours,' he said. 'And I haven't got the time to hang around.'

She was astounded to feel, for a second, a blip of disappointment.

Why not be wild for once . . . to derail that thought she asked, 'So how are you?'

'Great,' he replied 'I'm getting married. Next month.

At Marylebone Registry Office, over the road there.' He pointed.

'Wow.'

'And guess where we're having the reception?'

'The Winter Gardens?'

He said: 'You've got it. I don't want you to worry though. I've told my fiancée all about you . . . us and the thing, you know. She understands, she won't be annoyed or upset when we do it.'

'Well, I'm certainly still thinking about it. That was an incredible thing you did for me.'

He looked at her for what seemed like a long time.

'Yes it was.'

'Bye then.'

'Bye.'

THE LAST WOMAN KILLED IN THE WAR

Private Herbert Rawtenstall was his name. A conscript. At one minute to eleven o'clock on 11 November 1918, having made it unhurt through the mincing machine of Vimy Ridge, the Somme, Ypres, Herbert stuck his head over the edge of the trench, telling his sergeant he was 'going to take a shuftie about' and was hit square in the forehead by a sniper's bullet fired from the gun of a soldier of the Fourth Koenigsberg Regiment. The German pulled the trigger and felt the familiar kick of his Mauser rifle. Then a corporal came round the corner of his forward trench, tapped him on the shoulder and said, 'Manfred the war's over.'

'Oh yeah. Who won?' said Manfred and they both had a laugh about that. Then they went to the rear for some soup.

When Miss Owens told class 5A, the brightest girls at Queen Mary Grammar School, about the particularly pointless death of Private Rawtenstall, King's Own Lancashire

Rifleman, the last man killed in the First World War, it made Mary cry. The terrible sadness of it struck Mary very hard. She knew that Herbert was no more nor less dead than any of the other thirty-seven million soldiers done away with in that conflict but it was his coming so close to surviving that got to her.

If she hadn't heard about Herbert it was likely that she wouldn't have let the lad from the next street take her virginity at the age of sixteen. There was a Catholic youth club dance and the lad from the next street was in his uniform, looking all shy and none of the girls would go near him because although he wasn't strictly a darkie everybody knew his dad wasn't exactly white either. In the uniform of the King's Regiment (formerly the King's Own Lancashire Rifles) he could hardly fail to remind her of poor Herbert. Like Herbert he was unlucky in his timing too, being one of the very final batch of conscripts scooped up before that form of government shanghaiing ended in 1961. The boys and girls were strictly supervised but with a resourcefulness he would never show on the battlefield the lad found a cupboard where he and Mary grappled their way to a conclusion.

It took her five months to realise she was pregnant then she didn't know what else do do except tell her mum. Her mum told her dad.

The situation was so serious that they used the front parlour, which was always empty and smelt of cold.

Mary, her mum and her dad lived in Anfield, North End of Liverpool. Valley Road off Oakfield Road, ten terraced streets along from Liverpool Football Club's ground. On Saturdays the Corporation parked all the special buses for the match in their road and the kids made sixpence by storing men's bikes in their backyards. Liverpool Football Club were hoping to get promoted from the second division but Mary's dad said it would never happen. Mary's family were Catholics so they automatically supported Everton but anybody who wanted to be associated with success and elegant football would have backed Everton anyway because they were much the better team, lording it over the top of the first division, their ground Goodison Park rising high above Stanley Park.

All the houses in Valley Road were made of the same neat yellow brick and every day all the wives used to get down on their hands and knees and scrub their doorsteps with a stone to redden them. All the children played in the street and roamed far beyond in huge packs, riding buses and trains and ferries. If the kids went to Stanley Park, the ornate, verdant fields dotted with gothic sandstone park shelters, which separated Anfield from the mighty Everton ground, they would be watched over and handed from one network of appointed and self-appointed guardians to another, like a jetliner leaving the air traffic controllers of one country and entering another's. Any minor mischief the kids might want to commit had to evade the attention of the cocky park watchmen, the park police, various freelance old enforcers and, worst of all, spies, narks and finks within their own organisation. Kids who would run to an adult at the first sign of an infraction. If the children had their own aircraft controllers then so did the adults and in this crowded airspace the moral rules were very strict and ruthlessly enforced. The punishment was talking. Transgressors would cease to be talked to. Instead would be 'talked about'. Would suffer the terrible fate of being 'talked about in front of'. Women dreaded the inexplicable phrase, 'Some people are no better than they should be', being said pointedly across them in the bread queue of Scotts the Bakers. If that was said they would have to move. Bobby, the older brother of Jane Meacock, a classmate of Mary's, was found to be 'one of them', he was seen going into a pub in town where 'they' went. Jane's only option was not to speak to him ever again, she didn't. Mrs Noakes was divorced, she had been shunned for four years for this crime but had got her sentence commuted by ruthless orthodoxy ever since, indeed it was she who had dobbed Bobby in. Every Sunday night her ex-husband would wait at the top of the street for his daughter Barbara. 'Everything all right Barbara?' he would ask. She wouldn't speak but would hold out her hand for the five shillings he always gave her. He'd hand it over then she would turn and walk off. It was difference that was not tolerated, Mr Dixon used to beat his wife unconscious if Liverpool FC lost but 'You didn't interfere between a man and his wife'.

Oakfield Road, the main street that ran across the top of their road, was a busy thriving shopping street, in a busy thriving city. There were bakers, both independent and branches of chains, butchers ditto, three toy shops, the

Gaumont Cinema, a big Co-op store where your change whizzed about in brass canisters on overhead wires. At the other end of Valley Road there was a dairy with cows in it, Mary used to go there every day for milk and butter.

'A coon!' her dad shouted, 'it's bad enough that she's up the stick but to that nigger in the next street!' 'You've brought shame on us Mary,' said her mum, weeping. 'She'll have to go away,' her dad said. 'The shame'll kill me if the neighbours ever found out,' said her mum.

So the local priest was contacted and thus Mary was sent to an orphanage in Lancashire run by the Little Sisters of the Distressed Agatha. When her baby was born she didn't even get to look at its tiny face before it was taken away from her and put up for adoption. One of the kinder nuns whispered to her that she had given birth to a baby girl.

Mary sobbed for her mum but after three weeks the woman still had not come. She had to decide, alone, what to do with the rest of her life, not yet seventeen as she was. The nuns, women who never had sex and lived in a walled compound, blithely believed they had a profound knowledge of human nature and knew what was good for people. Plus they were losing ground to the enemy, not Satan but the Protestants, the Seventh Day Adventists and the Presbyterians in the vital battleground of the South Pacific. Mary was conscripted, she couldn't be a nun, of course, a lay worker then, for their missions abroad. In early 1962 Mary set sail by ship from the busy Liverpool docks to bring all the fun of Catholicism to the mud men of Papua New Guinea. And the mud women too.

It was a posting to the Somme just before the big push of 1918. Until the arrival of the missionaries most natives in PNG never left their village unless it was to wage war on another tribe or clan. All strangers were seen as enemies to be killed. The gimmick of the mud men of Asaro was that before a battle they coated themselves in mud so that their enemies thought the spirits had come to life. Conflicts occurred all the time, generally spiralling out of control in no time, this was because it was traditional that a wrong had to be answered with a massively greater retribution than the original wrong. For example, a pig in Mary's village had got loose and eaten some yams, a sacred vegetable, in a nearby village. Immediately, those villagers came and killed six people from the pig's village. If the Roman Catholic prelate hadn't stepped in a full-scale war would have broken out. After ten days of negotiations Mary's village agreed to slaughter twelve thousand pigs and war was avoided. There was only one other way out of warfare. Through the Kula Ring, islanders who might otherwise have spent all their days feuding and thus starved to death, instead twice a year exchanged elaborate shell necklaces and armbands. Sometimes a tribe that had been done an enormous wrong would, instead of waging war, make a massive gift to the perpetrator of the wrong, thus bringing terrible shame on them. Any PNG tribe preferred war, in which their children's limbs would be hacked off, to the massive gift.

Though it hardly seemed possible, in the last ten years Papua New Guinea had become an even more dangerous place. Many of the youths, alienated from their villages by schooling and exposure to the West, lacking the most rudimentary knowledge necessary to survive, such as which rot-resistant trees to use to build huts or which poisonous woods to avoid when making fires for cooking, became marauding 'rascals', they made Papua New Guinea's cities and roads the most hazardous in the world. Mary had been shot and robbed twice and had her scalp cut down to the skull by a machete.

After thirty-seven years the Little Sisters of the Distressed Agatha decided to switch Mary, who was ravaged by the after-effects of cholera, hepatitis A and hepatitis B so that she looked old and sad, whose English had withered away until she dreamed in Pidgin, back to Europe. She was told in a letter that she should make her way to an old people's home in Cheshire, they gave no reason why she was being moved, nuns are like that.

There was a change on to a small plane at Heathrow and this took her to Liverpool. She had known from the moment she had got the letter that she would visit Valley Road. Mary got a taxi (*teksi* in pidgin) from the rank outside and told it to go to Anfield. Air travel is so swift that you can leave yourself behind, on the runway or in the air. The most amazing sights if they appear on the road from the airport can be taken in without trouble, if mud men appeared at the Heathrow spur of the M4 they'd be surprised how little notice was taken of them. Mary had never really known the South End of the city anyway so it was no shock to her and as the taxi rode through the city centre she was able to say to herself with equanimity, 'Oh the whole of St John's Market's gone, thousands of houses round the cathedral vanished, gigantic empty spaces where London Road was.'

Along Oakfield Road 'the ground', Liverpool's stadium, seemed to have grown like some giant cane toad, squat and carbuncular and fed itself off the vitality of the whole area. All the shops had been burnt down or been bricked up or had big bites taken out of them, apart from a couple of Chinese chipshops (*yelopela sipstoa*). The only putting up seemed to have been road signs and little aluminium fences at every road junction and street corners, as if the inhabitants if not fenced in would fling themselves under the wheels of any passing car.

The cab could not turn into Valley Road since it was now a one way street, despite an almost complete absence of traffic, running the other way. So they had to drive down a parallel road then come back giving Mary a view of the whole street before they came to number five, the house where she had been born and cast out from. The neat conformity of the road had been replaced by construction anarchy, many houses had either been painted in bellowing colours or coated in strange materials: concrete with little stones in it or large slabs of pastel-hued paving blocks. Some had their bay windows removed to make the dwellings smaller for no good reason and replaced with flat plastic double glazing. Indeed every single house had different windows to the ones it had started life with and very few had their original roof slates instead being topped with cheap and porous red tiles.

Tranquillised by jet lag she knocked at number five. There was some shouting from inside after which the door was opened by a girl of perhaps eighteen, not quite white (*waitgil*) nor black (*blakgil*) with a silver spike through her nose.

'Yeah?' she asked.

Behind the coloured girl (*kalagil*) Mary could see that all the walls that had once divided the house into front parlour, back parlour, kitchen, pantry, had all gone. Instead it was one space, purple carpet on the floor that rose into various podia on which were seated small children staring at a giant TV.

'Yeah woh?' said the kalagil. Her accent was so thick that Mary had difficulty understanding what she was saying.

'Oh,' said Mary 'Mi . . . erm . . . I used to stop here years ago, we were the Maguire family then.'

'We still are,' said the girl 'Oor you?'

'My name is Mary Maguire.'

The girl peered closer into Mary's face then said 'Gran?' You, you're Granny Mary that went away.' Then she started shouting over her shoulder. 'Mam! Greatgran! Mam!'

Down the open staircase without banisters and through

the back door came two versions of Mary. An old grey-haired one in a purple velour track suit and a younger, darker, frizzier-haired one in a black T shirt and tight jeans, a jewel shining in the side of her nose. The older one reached the door and spoke.

'Mary?'

'Mum?'

'God girl, after all this time.' Then turning to the other woman, 'Shakira, it's yer mum.'

They brought Mary in and sat her on a hump of purple carpet.

'My daughter?'

'Yes Mary, your daughter Shakira.' She held the younger woman in front of her as if displaying the European Cup that was locked in a trophy cabinet half a mile up the road. Mary's mum's voice trembled with emotion. 'Grown into a fine strong woman of colour.'

(A woman of what?)

'Poor mite was in and out of foster homes, then the new legislation and all that comes in. Seventeen she was, turns up on me doorstep, looking all lost. Asking after her mum.'

A strange look at Mary then the two women smiled at each other over the memory of that special day.

'I took her in right away and when she got pregnant with little Kingsley, I took her in as well, gave them a home. Then those two little ones of Kingsley's come along . . . A house full of children. And now you're back . . . complete.'

Kingsley and her kids went and got Mary's luggage from

out of the taxi and brought it into the house. There seemed to be a million things to say but nobody wanted to start the avalanche. They had a meal instead to put something in their mouths to stop the big words coming out. Mary's mother who used to spend all day cooking gigantic stews and simmering ham hocks in split pea stocks now stuck a pile of Bird's Eye Potato Waffles in the microwave and served them 158 seconds later, half frozen and half burnt, covered in baked beans, to cries of satisfaction.

They told Mary about life in the street since she had left. Jane Meacock, whose brother Bobby had committed suicide, gave birth to a daughter by a Spanish sailor, Raleigh, six months after Mary. Her mum and dad made a fuss at first but 'when they saw the little baby their hearts melted'. Raleigh was married to a Rastafarian, though he couldn't come in the street any more because of an exclusion order. Mrs Noakes's scandalously divorced husband had moved back to the street with his male companion and Mrs Noakes had two more kids born from sperm donated by the husband's boyfriend. Mr Dixon who beat his wife was taken away by the police and Mrs Dixon, now sixty, shared her house with a woman called Bunty Redfern who smoked a pipe. There were many more tales of twisted lives, births, illnesses, deaths, babies, babies, babies.

Then they all went out. It was 'Granny Night' at the Sandown pub. Technically this event was restricted to women over forty but the bouncers on the door were happy to welcome Mary's mum, Shakira, Kingsley and their strange stiff friend. Inside the Sandown, which had once been split into a nest of little rooms reflecting the minute gradations of caste, saloon, public bar, smoking room, ladies' bar, four ale bar, was now one cavernous room filled with old women in sparkling clothes from out of home shopping catalogues. Mutton dressed as Joan Collins. They were all raucously drunk. Mary appeared out of place, she looked like what she was, an undercover nun. The three other Maguire women wove in and out of each other with the smooth love of long times spent together, they laughed, they joked, borrowed fags and Tampax from each other, said things that only they understood. Mary wished with all her heart that she was back with the mud men.

The main attraction of the night was some sort of troupe called the True Monty. To big band hits from the war years, four old men came on the stage dressed as Field Marshal Montgomery of Alamein, 'Monty'. They took their clothes off until they were completely naked then they came down into the audience, one old man wiggled his shrivelled member in front of Mary's mum's face, she laughed her head off.

After that they went back to the house in Valley Road.

There was vodka and supermarket own-brand Bailey's Irish Cream-type drink. Mary was more used to drinking fermented yams but she was no more or less drunk than the other women though her eyes swivelled and thoughts careered like go-karts around her skull – people tend to think this is the best state to be in to defuse the unexploded bomb of the past.

Mary's Mum started it. She turned to her daughter.

'God girl, this house was so empty when you ran away. I think that's what killed your dad, you running away like that.'

Mary seemed to be being accused of murder.

'I never ran away! I sat in that orphanage that you put me in, waiting for you to come and see me. You never came, you never came.'

'Mary love, we never put you in no orphanage.'

'You did, you did, you said the shame would kill you if the neighbours found out I was pregnant. Dad said the father was a coon!'

There was a hiss of disapproval from everybody at this including the two little ones. Mum spoke in a kind voice.

'Girl I don't know where you've been the last thirty years but we don't use that kind of racist language round here now and we never did, your blessed dad was no bigot.'

Shakira was looking at Mary in a very cold way, she was reminded of a documentary they had shown the mud men one Sunday during the very rainy season on their old 16mm projector. It was about the Second World War, the scene she recalled was a trial in Vichy France. A bewildered innocent man being hectored and falsely accused by a grim righteous skeleton of a judge who never paid for his crimes and died in his bed at a hundred and three years old, Shakira was that judge. A stranger she turned to explain herself to.

'Shakira . . . I was sent away, I wanted with all my heart

to keep you but I was only sixteen and girls couldn't have babies if they weren't married.'

'Was it the law?'

'Well no, but mum and dad cared what the neighbours thought.'

'Why would it have anything to do with the neighbours? Nobody judges anybody else round here.'

Mary's mum now, the prosecution's leading witness, 'Besides, Mary darling, if I cared about any of that why would I take Shakira in?'

Indeed why would she? Mary got up and ran sobbing out the door into Valley Road. 'There she goes again,' she heard her mum say as she fled.

She came to the gates of Stanley Park, silhouetted and twisted in the moonlight, raddled trees whispered behind the tortured iron. On the pavement one of the alloy fences had been hit by a van, a railing stuck out, its edge all sharp and jagged. A child already had had its face cut open. Mary pulled on the railing and dragged it free, then straightened it. She now held a short spear, formerly the weapon of choice in the Asaro Highlands until the cheap hunting rifles came from America. Climbing the gates and dropping down on to the silent path Mary slid across the bone-hard grass in a crouching run. She came to the boating lake, once it had bobbed with colourful rowing boats but when the Militant had been running Liverpool the genial old men who ran the lake had shown insufficient knowledge of Trotsky's disagreements with Stalin over the theory of Socialism in one country and so they'd drained the lake and made the old men care assistants in a halfway house for lesbian crack users. Now it was a muddy bowl. Mary took her clothes off and laid them at the edge of the lake. Some rainwater lay at the centre, the woman scooped some mud from the bottom of the lake and mixed it with the water until it was a thick paste. Then she smeared it on her body until she was the same grey colour all over. A mud woman stood in the moonlight in Stanley Park and raised her spear to the sky. A great wrong had been done to her, she had to avenge it, she would have to slaughter her mum, Shakira, Kingsley, the two little ones, Mrs Noakes . . . or she could buy them a speed boat.